COLT VS. COLT

"What did you say?" Dean asked, coming to his feet with his hands balled into fists.

"I said don't push me, Horse Face."

Dean's jaw dropped. Up to this point, Longarm had been the model of servitude. This talk just didn't fit the image he'd carefully crafted in order to lower their guard.

Dean brushed back the hem of his coat to expose a well-worn Colt. "You're gonna get down on your knees and beg for your worthless life or I'm gonna shoot you full of holes."

Longarm pushed back his own coat. He had a feeling that Dean was as fast with his gun as he was good with his fists. Either way, he was not a man to be taken lightly, and Longarm was going to have to either kill or completely humble the arrogant outlaw.

"If you want to spend the rest of your life in a pine box, make your play," Longarm said easily.

DON'T MISS THESE
ALL-ACTION WESTERN SERIES
FROM THE BERKLEY PUBLISHING GROUP

THE GUNSMITH by J. R. Roberts
Clint Adams was a legend among lawmen, outlaws, and ladies. They called him . . . the Gunsmith.

LONGARM by Tabor Evans
The popular long-running series about U.S. Deputy Marshal Long—his life, his loves, his fight for justice.

LONE STAR by Wesley Ellis
The blazing adventures of Jessica Starbuck and the martial arts master, Ki. Over eight million copies in print.

SLOCUM by Jake Logan
Today's longest-running action Western. John Slocum rides a deadly trail of hot blood and cold steel.

LONGARM

AND THE HELLDORADO KID

J

JOVE BOOKS, NEW YORK

LONGARM AND THE HELLDORADO KID

A Jove Book / published by arrangement with
the author

PRINTING HISTORY
Jove edition / April 1995

ISBN: 0-515-11591-6

A JOVE BOOK®
Jove Books are published by The Berkley Publishing Group,
200 Madison Avenue, New York, New York 10016.
JOVE and the "J" design are trademarks
belonging to Jove Publications, Inc.

PRINTED IN THE UNITED STATES OF AMERICA

10 9 8 7 6 5 4 3 2 1

LONGARM

AND THE
HELLDORADO KID

Chapter 1

Longarm removed the half-chewed cheroot from the corner of his mouth and batted a cloud of trail dust from his pants. He knew he looked rough, but he'd just returned from Arizona and had gotten a message to hurry into the Denver headquarters just as soon as he arrived back in town.

"Mr. Billy Vail wants to see you right away. Important business," was the terse message that had been given to Longarm by his hotel manager.

Longarm knocked on Billy's door, curious about what could be so important that it could not wait until a tired, dirty, and hungry lawman had a few hours to rest and eat after being gone for six weeks.

"Come in!" Billy called.

Longarm entered the office and trod wearily across the hardwood floor to take a seat in front of Billy's desk. His boss looked harried and irritable, with piles of papers scattered about his desk in complete disorder.

"Buried up to your eyeballs in paperwork as usual?" Longarm teased.

"Damn right," Billy growled, looking up for the first time to see Deputy Custis Long. "Man, you look like a horse that's been spurred up and down Pike's Peak."

"I feel like one," Longarm said, crossing his legs and thumbing back the brim of his black Stetson hat. "And I'm looking forward to a long-overdue vacation."

"I'm sure you are," Billy said, appearing genuinely concerned. "I'd say you've lost about twenty pounds since I saw you last. Hell, Custis, you even *look* older."

Longarm stuffed his annoyance. "I am older and so are you, Billy. Now what is so damned important that it couldn't wait a few days?"

Billy pushed back from his chair and stood up. He massaged his eyes with thumb and forefinger, then placed his hands in the small of his back and applied pressure with a groan.

"Damn," he said, "I swear that sitting at a desk is three times worse on your back than sitting on a horse."

"Then take a demotion and come join the rest of us poor devils back out in the field," Longarm said without even the pretense of sympathy.

"You're a hard man, Custis."

"I'm a hungry and tired man." Longarm was in no mood for small talk. "What is it this time, Billy?"

"I've got a problem that needs my best deputy."

Longarm wasn't about to be suckered by flattery, not in his current foul mood. "Too bad, Billy, because I've got a problem that needs about a week of rest."

"Maybe I can give you a few days."

"I need a week."

Billy glanced at his desk calendar, considered it thoughtfully, and then said, "I just might be able to give you four days."

Longarm jammed the cigar back into his mouth. "Tell me your big problem and don't exaggerate, as usual."

Billy massaged the small of his back for a moment as he circled the room. Physically, he was the exact opposite of Longarm. He was short, heavyset, and slightly balding. He looked soft and bookish, but Longarm knew that he was really quite strong, and had distinguished himself in the field as an honest and fearless deputy United States marshal before he had been promoted to a paper-pushing desk job.

Billy stopped at his office window and gazed out across Denver toward the distant snowcapped Rocky Mountains. "Man, oh, man," he said, "every time I look up at those magnificent peaks, I think about the time that I chased Cut-Faced Jack Hooleran and his gang."

"Billy," Longarm told him, "I've heard that story about ten times and I'm just too damned tired and hungry to sit here and listen to it again. Okay?"

Billy turned away from the window. He wore a hurt expression. "Ten times? I doubt that."

"All right," Longarm conceded, "seven or eight. What's the tough job?"

Billy flopped back down in his desk chair. "Did you ever hear of a town called Helldorado?"

"Yeah." Longarm's brow knitted. "I believe that's in Arizona, isn't it?"

"Not even close. It's in western Nevada. About fifteen miles east of Carson City."

"Okay," Longarm said. "I know the lay of that land. But the last time I was through there, I remember a town called Dayton, and then a few miles east of that you come to Fort Churchill."

"Helldorado is south of them both."

3

"Now that," Longarm said, "has just gotta be hard, dry country."

Billy nodded. "That's about the only kind of place you'll find any gold or silver strikes anymore. All the scenic or even hospitable country has been mined to death. You can't find much ore up in the Rockies or the Sierras because they've already been prospected so heavily."

"Tell me about Helldorado," Longarm said.

"It used to be a booming town. At least on the surface that's what it appeared to be."

"What does that mean?"

"They did strike gold and silver there. A couple of hundred thousand dollars worth, I'm told. But as quickly as the boom started, it went bust."

"Borrasca," Longarm said.

"What?"

"It's a Spanish word the Mexicans on the Comstock Lode use for mines that won't pay or suddenly go bust. It kind of means 'bad luck' or 'barren rock.' *Borrasca* is the opposite of *bonanza,* 'a rich strike.' "

"Thanks for the Spanish lesson," Billy said cryptically. "Now, can I go on with the story of Helldorado?"

"I quiver with eagerness to hear it," Longarm said with a touch of a smile.

"All right. Helldorado apparently went *borrasca* a few years ago. The town withered, and it was bought by a man by the name of Matthew Killion. Heard of him?"

"Yeah," Longarm said, "he's owned some big mines on the Comstock. At least, they looked big on paper. But I heard that Killion was far better at mining the pockets of stock market speculators than he ever was the mines themselves."

4

"That's true. I've been told that the man is totally unscrupulous. When Killion and his boys ran out of suckers, they started an extortion ring that put the pinch on the remaining merchants in Helldorado."

"What about the town marshal?"

"He was said to be either in cahoots with Killion and his boys, or else just too afraid of them to do much about it. The upshot of the thing was that a vigilante committee was formed with the express purpose of lynching Killion and his gang of thieves. I guess that Killion has two sons and the older one is lightning fast with a six-gun."

"And the younger?"

"He's probably just as bad. I've always said that snakes beget snakes."

"Sure," Longarm said. "So what happened? Did Killion and his crowd run for their lives?"

"That's right," Billy said. "They bluffed and threatened but, when it became obvious that half the town was ready to lynch them, the Killion gang vanished like smoke in the wind. Rumor has it that they robbed a few trains and stagecoaches over in California and roosted for a while in San Francisco."

"That's a wild enough town for men like that," Longarm said. "They could get away with a lot over there before they got people riled up enough to stretch their necks."

"Well, they did and people almost did," Billy said. "Vigilantes came for them one night in San Francisco too, but they all got away again and they went straight back to Nevada. By that time Helldorado was damn near deserted. They drove everybody else out of the place and made it their headquarters. They've been raising hell ever since. We think they robbed the Union Pacific Railroad just east of Donner Pass and got away with about ten thousand dollars."

"Wow!" Longarm said with a whistle. "Any witnesses to identify them?"

"No," Billy said. "It was an inside job. They must have bribed one of the guards, because he got the jump on the others and had them lie face down on the floor of the mail car while the gang boarded and cleaned out the safe and all the federal money orders."

"So that's where we come in. A federal offense was committed and they crossed state lines."

"Exactly," Billy said. "And they got away clean with nary a witness. Or if there was a witness, he was too frightened to speak up."

"And they rode straight back to Helldorado to live happily ever after."

"How did you guess?" Billy asked. "That's exactly what they did."

"So I'm supposed to go to Helldorado and . . . and what? If there were no witnesses, how can I make an arrest?"

"You can't," Billy conceded. "What you'd have to do is to infiltrate the gang. Pretend to be an outlaw on the run looking for like-minded men."

"I see." Longarm laced his fingers behind his head. "And then get the goods on the bunch of 'em."

"That's it," Billy said. "It shouldn't be that difficult for a man who possesses your ingenuity."

"It'll be a sonofabitch and we both know it," Longarm said flatly. "In the first place, I run the very real risk of someone recognizing me. And in the second place, I'll probably have to 'prove' myself by doing something illegal. Maybe even participating in a robbery or a murder."

6

"I know," Billy said, his smile dying. "I've thought of little else but that possibility, and I know that I can't offer you any easy answers. You will, in all probability, have to ride with this gang and take part in whatever they are up to in order to earn their trust. But it will be worth it."

"Not to me. Not if it puts innocent people's lives in danger."

Billy came to his feet again and began to pace back and forth. "If it were me, I'd think of some way to help their victims rather than be a bystander or even a participant."

" 'Help' them?"

"Sure! Maybe you can save lives."

Longarm supposed there was some logic to this.

"Custis, these are real hardcases. They've not only robbed, but they've killed. We need to stop them and the sooner the better. You can understand that, can't you?"

"Well sure, but . . ."

"I need you to leave tomorrow morning," Billy said, coming to stand before Longarm.

Longarm bounced to his feet. "No! Absolutely not. I'm worn to the bone, Billy. Even you said that I looked awful."

"I didn't mean it."

"Yes, you did. But a few days of rest will fix me up just fine."

Billy jammed his hands into his coat pockets. "Tell you what I think we can do. We'll give you *a first-class ticket* from Cheyenne to Reno. That way, you'll get your five days' rest on the train. You'll have your own luxurious sleeping compartment and the finest meals that money can buy. You'll even have the opportunity to order free champagne with your five-course dinner. How does that sound?"

"It sounds like I'm going to need to buy some nicer clothes and a much better brand of cigar. How about a hundred dollars extra expense money just so that I can look like I belong in first class instead of the cattle car?"

"Fair enough," Billy agreed. "But I never thought you'd stoop so low that you'd screw the government when you had it over a barrel."

"Well," Longarm said, "that just goes to show how little you really understand me. The fact of the matter is that I have no problem at all with taking a little gravy on my potatoes. Not when this agency is sending me into a situation that is likely to get me killed."

"Be an optimist."

"I'm a realist," Longarm retorted. "I don't believe in fairy tales, and I don't believe in the lucky rabbit's foot either. You're putting me into something that no other man in this agency would accept."

Billy's congenial smile melted. "Nobody else working out of this federal office is nearly as good as you, Custis."

"Stow it," Longarm said, thinking that he could at least get one night's good rest before boarding the train tomorrow morning. "And get the money—all of it."

"You sound as if you are planning to take the money and run."

"It would be the intelligent thing to do."

"Custis, this job won't be tough at all for you. Why, you've just come back from a far worse ordeal in Arizona."

"Just requisition my expense money and cut the bull-shit," Longarm said. "My gut is growling and I need to buy some better clothes for the trip west. I just hope that no one recognizes me."

"Shave off your mustache."

"That won't do anything."

"Just a thought," Billy said with a shrug of his round shoulders. "Just a thought."

Longarm nodded, and watched as Billy brought out the forms to order his travel money and first-class ticket. It would be nice to travel in style for a change. He'd need a shave, a haircut, and those new clothes. And some expensive cigars. Yeah, Longarm thought, this could even work out pretty nice, if things didn't suddenly turn fatal.

Chapter 2

The ice was two inches deep on the water troughs the next morning. Longarm didn't care. His first-class ticket would afford him a rare five days of comfort after he boarded the Denver Pacific Railroad, whose 106-mile line would deliver him to Cheyenne. From Cheyenne, he would transfer into another first-class berth on the Union Pacific, which would carry him in luxury all the way to Reno.

Longarm did not appear to be at all the same man who had ridden into Denver the previous morning sore, tired, and dirty from a long, hard ride up from Arizona. In fact, those who had seen the tall, haggard deputy marshal would not even recognize him as the well-to-do-looking gentleman who now held a first-class ticket in his hand and wore a new suit, new black Stetson, and new boots. Longarm had spent most of his extra government money on his clothes, but he figured he was worth it. Besides, he could never have traveled first-class looking like a saddle bum without attracting a great deal of attention.

"Why, Marshal Long!" the conductor said as Custis

boarded the train. "I hardly recognized you and—"

"*Don't* recognize me, Jess. Okay?" Longarm pulled the conductor up the aisle where they could not be overheard. "You see, I'm sort of traveling incognito."

"Incog what?" Jess asked, his face a complete blank.

"I'm sort of traveling in disguise, Jess. I'm traveling first-class, and I'd appreciate it if you'd just act like I was your ordinary successful and wealthy businessman, rancher, or politician. You understand?"

Jess had been a conductor on this line since its start in 1870 and he was a fixture. Long past normal retirement age, the old gent was extremely popular both among the passengers and the other railroad employees.

But right now, he was confused. "Why, sure, but . . . well, what am I supposed to call you?"

"Mr. Long. Not Marshal, or Longarm, or even Custis, because that would be too informal if I'm supposed to be a prominent businessman."

"All right," Jess said, "but everyone else on this train is going to be callin' out 'Longarm' or 'Deputy,' and I don't hardly see how you can stop 'em."

"Maybe it isn't even necessary until I get on the Union Pacific," Longarm said. "But let's just start pretending right now. Okay?"

"Why sure, Cust . . . Mr. Long."

"Good." Longarm gave the man his first-class ticket. "I'll expect the best of your service, just like everyone else in first class."

The conductor stared at the ticket. "Is this costing us taxpayers?" he asked with a frown.

"I'm afraid so, although it's only an additional forty-three dollars over the second-class fare between Cheyenne and Reno," Longarm said, understanding the

11

old man's disapproval. "And I'll let you in on a little secret."

Jess's pale and watery blue eyes widened and he grinned. "What is it?"

"I'm going to recover a bunch of stolen taxpayers' money and that's why I have to spend a little extra on this first-class ticket."

"How much are you going to recover?"

"I can't tell you that, Jess. But at least a hundred times what it's costing the taxpayers to send me to Reno."

"That's where you're going?"

Longarm nodded.

"Then you must be after that ten thousand dollars that was stolen off the Union Pacific Railroad a couple of months ago up near Donner Pass!"

"Shhh!" Longarm put his finger to his lips. "Dammit, Jess, I don't want any of this leaking out. Do you understand me?"

"Well, sure!" Jess vowed, looking slightly offended. "I know how to keep my mouth shut."

"I know that," Longarm said, wanting to mollify the conductor. "Now just keep all of this under your cap and we'll both be a lot better off."

"I'll do it, and I'll tell your first-class porter and the dining room staff not to call out your name."

"I'd appreciate that," Longarm said with relief. "I'm sure that a few of my fellow first-class passengers will also transfer at Cheyenne and proceed on to Reno. When I get to Nevada, I hope to go about my investigation without anyone knowing who I am."

"It'd help if you shaved off that mustache and got a haircut."

"I got a haircut just yesterday."

"A real *short* haircut, Marsh . . . I mean, Mr. Long. The fellas with money have their hair cut a whole lot shorter than you."

"So do prison convicts," Longarm said. He removed his new black-felt Stetson. "Fine hat, isn't it?"

"It sure is, but it looks just like your old one, only it's new. You should have bought a derby."

"I *hate* derbies and bowlers," Longarm said with considerable passion. "They look like soup bowls turned upside down on a fella's head. The little bitty brim is worthless for keeping the sun out of a man's eyes, and it'll allow the back of a horseman's neck to get burned to a crisp."

"Yeah, only people with money don't much ride horses, Custis. They ride carriages."

The old man had a good point, which Longarm chose to ignore. "You're to call me Mr. Long, remember?"

"Sorry."

"Never mind. Just give me a good berth and tell my porter that he'd better address me as Mr. Long and give me as good a service as if I'd paid for this first-class ticket out of my own pocket."

"I will, but I sure hate to see the taxpayers pay for that ticket. You gonna pay 'em back if you don't recover the money?"

Longarm was getting irritated. "No," he said shortly. "This conversation is over, Jess."

"Sure," the conductor said. "I got other first-class passengers coming. And all of them have paid for their *own* first-class tickets."

"Well, good for them!"

"And one of 'em is a duchess or a princess or some such thing."

13

"You don't say."

Jess nodded vigorously. "She's from England and of royal blue blood."

"Have you seen her?"

"Yep," Jess said.

Longarm had never met royalty before and he thought it would be interesting. "What's she like?"

"She's beautiful, just like you'd expect of an English princess."

Longarm became even more interested. "About how old is the woman?"

"I'd judge her to be in her mid-twenties."

"Traveling with a prince, I suppose?"

"Nope, traveling alone except for some old biddy who is bossy as hell. Mrs. Addie is her name, and I can already see that she's going to give us all fits. She wants everything perfect for the princess. We had to do a lot of shuffling around to give them adjoining berths, the two largest and nicest on the train. The ones we use when the president of this line travels to and from Cheyenne."

"How about that," Longarm said, very impressed. "I hope I get a chance to meet this princess. Any idea why she is traveling to Cheyenne?"

"She's bound for San Francisco."

"Good," Longarm said, "then I'll have plenty of time to get acquainted with her."

"I doubt that Mrs. Addie will even let you near the princess," Jess said. "You might be wearing new clothes, but she'll see that six-shooter strapped to your waist and she'll know that you're not a gentleman."

"Well," Longarm said, "perhaps I'll leave my sidearm locked in my sleeping compartment."

14

"You'd do that given all the enemies you've made as a United States marshal?"

"Will anyone else in the first-class coach be wearing a six-gun?"

"No, but . . . well, you *are* a deputy United States marshal, and I'm sure there are plenty of folks who'd like to put a slug through your gizzard."

"I didn't say that I'd be *completely* disarmed."

The conductor looked relieved. "Glad to hear that," he said. "I was worried for a minute."

Longarm patted the kindly old gent on the shoulder. "You just worry about Mrs. Addie. I'll take care of myself, and it will help a lot if you warn the other staff about the fact that I'm traveling incognito."

"Means in disguise, right?"

"Right." Longarm grinned. "Jess, which compartment have they reserved for me?"

Jess consulted a clipboard with a roster of compartment assignments. "Uh-oh," he said.

"What's wrong?"

"You got the small one."

"The small one?"

"Yes, it used to be used by the porter who took care of our first-class passengers. But the railroad wanted to squeeze a few more pennies of profit so they converted it to a private first-class compartment."

"Humph," Longarm snorted, not liking the sound of this.

"I wouldn't be too upset," Jess said. "After all, you'll only have to put up with it for today. Since you've only got it up to Cheyenne, you'll probably want to just stay in the parlor car."

Longarm was not pleased. "Well, for crying out loud,"

15

he complained. "I would have thought that, for the price of a first-class ticket, I wouldn't have to put up with that sort of inconvenience."

"Well," Jess said, "that compartment has a sizeable discount. In fact, it doesn't cost the government a cent more than a second-class compartment."

Longarm realized that Billy Vail had snookered him one more time. "Show me the way."

Jess hailed a porter who was not all that much younger than himself. "Hello, Arnold."

"Hi, Longarm." Arnold eyed him up and down, and then he clucked his tongue and said, "Boy, you sure are gussied up!"

"Explain that incognito thing I'm doing to him later," Longarm told Jess. "Right now, I just want to flop down in my private car and take a long nap."

"Arnold, Mr. Long has been assigned compartment five," Jess said to his underling.

"I doubt he'll even fit in that one," the porter said. "You know how small it is."

Longarm groaned. Things were not getting off to the good start that he'd anticipated. Still, the conductor was right, it was only one day. The Denver Pacific wasn't nearly as well financed as the Union Pacific, and perhaps he shouldn't have expected luxury on this very short northern run to Cheyenne.

But a few minutes later when Arnold opened the door to his private compartment, Longarm was appalled. "Why, you couldn't stuff a kid and a chipmunk in this place!"

"I'm sorry," Arnold said. "I told Jess that you were far too big a man for this sleeping compartment."

"Take me to the parlor car," Longarm ordered.

"You'll like that a lot better." Arnold promised.

Longarm followed Arnold up the aisle and into the parlor car reserved for first-class passengers only.

"This is more like it," he growled, flopping down in a plush wine-colored seat beside a window that was actually clean enough to see through. "How about a glass of champagne before we get under way?"

"Very good," Arnold said, disappearing into the dining car.

Longarm leaned back and sighed. He could nap just fine in this big, soft seat and just watch the world drift by. He twisted a little to get more comfortable, and realized that he was still wearing his big .44-.40 Colt Model T revolver. If the princess and Mrs. Addie suddenly appeared, they'd see that big gun and it might scare them off.

"Be right back!" Longarm called out to Arnold as he returned to his tiny compartment, where his bags were waiting.

He stepped inside the cramped little cubicle, removed his six-gun, and put it into his sturdy leather handcase. Then, he made sure that his vest-pocket derringer was in good firing order. The weapon was unique and had proven its value time and time again. It was attached by a gold chain to his Ingersoll watch, which rested in his other vest pocket. The derringer was a neat little .44-caliber with twin barrels. It was not very accurate, but then accuracy was irrelevant in the confines of a railroad car or when closely confronting an enemy in a saloon.

The derringer had never failed Longarm, and he'd used it many times to catch opponents off guard when they thought he was merely reaching for his pocket watch to learn the time of day. Satisfied that the derringer was loaded and ready for action in the unlikely event it would suddenly be needed, Longarm studied himself in a small mirror. He looked so impressive that he wondered if he actually should have pursued money and power instead of the excitement and the satisfaction that were the rewards of men in his dangerous profession.

"Perhaps," he told himself, "I'll find a new line of endeavor one of these days and make some *real* money."

But even as he said this, Longarm knew that he wasn't serious. He loved being a lawman and he was very, very good at it, just as Billy Vail had told him yesterday.

Longarm cast aside his foolish thoughts of wealth and business. He couldn't stand finance and he had no head for figures. No, Longarm decided, unless he married money or discovered it buried deep in a mine shaft, he was probably going to be a poor workingman the rest of his life.

Longarm straightened his tie, combed his hair with his fingers, and headed back to the parlor car. He was somewhat disappointed, however, to see that an older woman with her hair in a severe bun had chosen his empty seat. No matter, there were plenty of others by the windows.

Longarm took a seat as far away from the woman as he could get, guessing that this might be the obstreperous Mrs. Addie whom the conductor had warned him about. The porter brought him a glass of champagne, and Longarm wondered if he was supposed to tip the man or if this kind of sterling service was figured into the price of the first-class fare.

"I say, sir, I overheard the conductor telling his porter

that you are a United States marshal. Is this actually true? Are you really a federal marshal of the Old West?"

Longarm turned around to face the woman. He was annoyed that even this woman knew his true identity. "Before I answer that, are you Mrs. Addie?"

"I am."

She was a sharp-featured woman, with an aquiline nose, very pale and powdered complexion, and perfect white teeth. The diamonds in her earrings were no doubt worth more than Longarm's accumulated pension. The woman surprised him greatly when she left her seat and came over to join him.

She extended a gloved hand and shook his hand firmly, saying, "My name is Mrs. Lucille Buckmeister Addie, and may I ask yours, Marshal?"

"Custis Long. And the marshal part was supposed to be a secret."

The woman, whom Longarm judged to be in her sixties, raised her brows in surprise. "It was?"

"Yes," he said, "it was. But I guess that there's no such thing as a secret on this train, is there, Arnold?"

The porter, who had been hovering close by, looked at Longarm with the innocence of a small child. "Were you addressing me, sir?"

"Of course I was!"

"Don't be nasty with the poor man," Addie said. "I'm sure that he is paid wretchedly by this miserable little railroad and has never been educated."

Arnold didn't like that comment, but he was too well trained to protest. "Can I get you anything, Mrs. Addie?"

"Champagne," she said airily.

Longarm squirmed in his seat feeling trapped. Mrs. Addie might be part of the royal family of England, but her perfume was strong enough to kill swarming Montana mosquitos at sixty paces.

"Custis Long?"

"Yes, ma'am."

"What a quaint name? English, isn't it?"

"I suppose."

Addie looked curiously at him. "You don't even know your family tree?"

"Nope."

Mrs. Addie looked appalled. "How . . . how tragic!"

"Why?" Longarm asked. "I know that my folks had nothing and that I'll not inherit anything. And as for being English or Irish or French, who cares?"

"Are you serious?"

"Sure I am."

"My God," the woman said, shaking her head and looking upset, "you Westerners certainly do have queer attitudes about your origins and bloodlines."

"Bloodlines don't mean anything in the American West," Longarm said with conviction.

"I don't believe that!" Mrs. Addie fell silent, but when her champagne arrived, she looked up at Arnold and said, "Bring us the entire bottle, you ignorant fool."

Arnold's cheeks reddened and he stomped up the aisle.

"You had no right to speak to Arnold that way," Longarm admonished. "Arnold isn't a fool, and people out in this country won't stand being insulted."

"Humph!"

"It's true," Longarm said. "And you can also forget about bloodlines and pedigrees. Out here, most of us are a bunch of mavericks."

"What, pray tell, are 'mavericks'?"

"They're unbranded calves," Longarm explained. "They're free and tied to no one. They don't carry any markings or respect any boundaries. Those men who aren't mavericks probably consider themselves mustangs."

"Those are your wild scrub horses," Mrs. Addie stated, looking quite pleased with this bit of knowledge, probably gained from one of the colorful and totally sensationalized travel brochures put out by the Union Pacific and other railroads to promote travel into the untamed American frontier as an adventure. "I've heard of those."

"And what have you heard?"

"That they are indeed running wild but that they are unfit for a rider who expects even a little quality."

"That's not true," Longarm said, "I've ridden a great many mustang ponies and—"

"And who are you?" the young woman who had suddenly appeared asked.

"I'm Custis Long," Longarm said, his eyes filled with the radiance of her beauty. "And you must the princess."

"I'm afraid that my title is much less impressive than a princess. I am Lady Caroline, but please just call me Caroline. May I join you?"

Longarm jumped out of his seat. Caroline was stunning, with long, light brown hair, blue eyes, a flawless complexion, and a perfectly radiant smile.

"He's a United States Marshal," Mrs. Addie announced proudly.

"Sit down," Caroline said happily as she took a seat beside Longarm. "I wanted to hear what you had to say about wild mustangs. We are so hoping that we might be able to see a few from the train."

"Not very likely," Longarm said. "Mustangs are too smart to come near our towns or railroads. Those that did have long since been shot or captured."

"What a disappointment," Caroline said. "And just a few minutes ago the conductor told me that I could not really hope to see any wild Indians riding across your vast but hostile American plains, mountains, and deserts."

"You might see a few Indians," Longarm said, not wishing to completely disappoint the woman, "but they'll be anything but wild. You'll see plenty of them in Cheyenne and most all the rail towns we pass through. Some of them even work for the railroad and the freighting companies."

"But . . . but there are no more free-roaming ones?"

"Only a few Apache are still free to come and go as they wish," Longarm explained. "Geronimo is still raising hell down in the Arizona Territory, but he's on his last legs and General George Cook is about to tighten the noose and drag him back to the reservation."

"That's a place where they are kept?"

"A reservation is land that the government has given the Indians to live on."

"But didn't they already own all this land?" Caroline asked innocently.

"Yes," Longarm admitted, realizing his poor choice of words, "but now the government is giving pieces of it back to the Indians and trying to teach them how to farm and raise livestock."

"I can't imagine your wild Indians as farmers."

"That's the problem," Longarm said. "They can't

either. They're free-ranging hunters and they like to keep moving with the herds and the seasons. Unfortunately, our buffalo herds are about wiped out and the Indians are supposed to stay on their reservations."

"It sounds as if they are probably quite unhappy," Caroline said.

"That's a fair statement."

"Tell me about those scrubby mustangs," Mrs. Addie said, interrupting.

"Well," Longarm began, "like I said, those horses are free and rootless, like most Western men. And like the miners and the cowboys, the loggers and freighters, they're a little rough-looking."

"Jug-headed?" Mrs. Addie asked.

"Some are."

"Runty?"

"They're not nearly as tall as your English race horses," Longarm admitted, "but a thoroughbred or an English saddlebred wouldn't last a month out on the dry and harsh ranges of Nevada where our own mustangs thrive."

"Why not?" Caroline asked. "We have severe winters in England."

"And I'll bet you bring those fancy horses into the barn when the weather turns especially foul."

"Yes, of course, but—"

Longarm thought he was probably out of line to interrupt even a lady, but he did it anyway. "Well, while your horses are in a barn munching oats, the mustang is suffering with ice in his ears and coat and his tail to the wind. He's eating bark to stay alive and fighting off wolves and cougars that are trying to trap and pull him

23

down in the heavy, driving snow."

"I see your point," Caroline said. "Yes, you are right, our English purebreds would never survive given those cruel circumstances."

"The mustang is small and often of poor conformation," Longarm admitted, "but he's tough, resourceful, and if you can find one young enough to break, they make wonderful horses with an endurance that is unmatched."

"I do so want to see one," Caroline gushed. "Is there any chance, Marshal, that you could be persuaded to escort us into the wild to view a band of these little horses?"

"I'm afraid not," Longarm said, "though I'd like to. Fact is, I've got a job to do in Reno. But you can find any number of guides who would take you out to see the mustangs. Nevada is full of them."

"Then we'll do that!" Caroline said, her voice filled with excitement. "What do you think, Lucille?"

"I think it's a crazy idea and that we ought to go straight on to San Francisco just as planned."

"Oh." Caroline's spirits drooped noticeably. "Well, we'll see."

"It'd probably only take you a day or two at most to see mustangs," Longarm said. "And maybe I could find a spare day and you could go with me, if you'd feel safer."

"That would be wonderful!" Caroline exclaimed. "I mean, you are a real officer of the law, aren't you?"

"I am."

"Then I hope that we can do it."

Longarm leaned back in his chair and felt positively wonderful. "Champagne?" he asked the ladies.

"Yes," Mrs. Addie said with a fair degree of enthusiasm.

"I'll have some too," Caroline said.

"Porter?" Longarm called.

Arnold suddenly appeared. "Yes, Marshal?"

"Champagne all around, please."

"Very good, sir."

A few minutes later, Longarm raised his new glass of champagne. "To your health, ladies."

"And to yours," Caroline said, eyes shining with excitement as they drank the excellent vintage. "May I ask you one small question?"

"Of course."

"Why aren't you armed? We've seen several lawmen since leaving Omaha and they've all carried your famous six-guns. I hope that some bad man does not recognize and shoot you."

"I don't think there are many that travel the railroad as first-class passengers, Caroline."

"Perhaps not," she said. "But I have read how little value some of your Western outlaws place on human life, and your vulnerability concerns me."

"Then the next time we meet, I'll be wearing my six-gun," he told her. "The truth of the matter was that I felt it might alarm you ladies and so I left it in my compartment."

"I'd like to see your big gun later," Caroline said, looking quite excited. "Has it actually been used in a . . . how do you call it, a shootout?"

"Yes, and I promise you," Longarm said, gazing deep into the azure pools of her lovely eyes, "before we get to Reno you shall see my big gun."

Caroline just smiled and sipped the champagne, but

Mrs. Addie, older and wiser, had caught a hint of Longarm's lecherous intentions and she was no longer smiling.

I am, Longarm warned himself, going to have be more careful if I want to fool this old crone and make love to royalty. Much, much more careful.

Chapter 3

After the champagne and a long and sumptuous feast with Lady Caroline and her watchdog, the suspicious Mrs. Addie, Longarm tromped back to his cramped little compartment and wedged himself into an S-shape in preparation for a long nap. He was still very tired, and knew that he needed to physically replenish himself for whatever ordeal awaited him in Nevada.

"But I will make it a point to take Lady Caroline out to see the mustangs north of Reno," Longarm mumbled just before he drifted off to sleep about forty miles north of Denver. "And maybe I can manage to lose Mrs. Addie, or at least see that she is captured by some friendly Paiute Indians."

Longarm slept until well after sunset, when he was awakened by the train blasting its whistle announcing its arrival in Cheyenne.

"Cheyenne station!" came the porter's call. "Everybody prepare to unload."

Longarm shook the cobwebs from his mind and forced himself into a sitting position. He struggled to his feet.

It took several minutes for him to come fully awake. Finally, he reached for his hat, gun, and holster. By the time he was able to collect his gear and get outside on the station platform, Lady Caroline and Mrs. Addie were already speeding off toward one of the hotels in a rented carriage.

Longarm wasn't pleased. Not only had he missed the opportunity of dining a second time with the lovely Caroline, but he'd also lost the chance to squire her around Cheyenne and maybe, just maybe, end up in her royal embrace.

"Well, it'll take four nights for this train to get us to Reno, more if I get lucky and the damn thing breaks down," Longarm muttered to himself.

"Marshal, good luck to you on that Donner Pass train robbery," Arnold said.

"For the love of Mike, do you know about that too?"

Arnold shrugged and worked up a smile. "Sure. Jess told me. I hope that you find them thievin' bastards. You know, they pistol-whipped one of the Union Pacific mail room clerks when he was slow handing over the federal accounts. Pistol-whipped him so bad he's still unconscious and not expected to live."

"I didn't hear about that," Longarm said.

"Well, you can bet that every railroad man on every line west of the Mississippi River has heard about it and we're all pulling for you, Longarm."

"Does *everyone* on this train know about my business in Nevada?"

"I expect so," Arnold said proudly. "And there's little doubt that the telegraph operator will send the message along to Reno and east to Omaha and—"

Longarm swore in frustration. "That's the very last

28

thing that I wanted to happen! The entire reason I've bought new clothes and am traveling first-class is that I'm supposed to be traveling incognito."

"Yeah, that's what Jess said. But it'll never work, Marshal. Too many people know you 'cause you've been comin' and goin' on the Union Pacific for too many years."

In his heart, Longarm suspected this was the truth. The only comforting thing was that he'd be leaving Reno and riding out into the barren hills of Nevada to find Helldorado and Matthew Killion's gang of thieves. Perhaps they wouldn't recognize him and he could be among them just long enough to get enough evidence to make his arrests.

"Arnold, did you happen to hear where Lady Caroline was spending the night?"

"Probably at the Winston House. That's the fanciest boardinghouse in Cheyenne."

"Yeah," Longarm said, "I suppose that it is."

"Good-lookin', isn't she!"

"No doubt about that."

"Marshal, I wonder if she . . ." Arnold's cheeks turned red with embarrassment and the porter could not continue. "Aw, never mind."

"What?"

"Well, you know."

"No," Longarm said, "I don't. What are you wondering about?"

"Well, if she . . . you know."

Longarm had to work not to keep from smiling. "You mean if she's any *different physically* because she's from a royal family?"

"That, and if she . . . you know, enjoys a man in bed."

29

Longarm shrugged. "I'll be honest with you, Arnold. I never even met a royal lady and I don't know what they do in bed. But when you get right down to the basics, royalty are human beings just like the rest of us commoners."

"Do you really think so?"

"Why, sure! Royalty are just people that either happened to be born to their high stations or married into it. Either way, it don't give them the right to put on superior airs. I judge folks by what they do, not the title that goes before their names."

"I dunno," Arnold said, looking very skeptical. "I never seen a woman to equal Lady Caroline."

"She's beautiful and gracious and probably rich," Longarm conceded, "but she's still just a person like the rest of us and I'll bet she has the same needs, fears, and even desires."

"Then you don't expect that it's sort of . . . well, beneath the royal dignity of a woman like that to have a good romp in the sack?"

"Nope," Longarm said with conviction. "I sure don't. Arnold, I fully expect that Lady Caroline enjoys a man every bit as much as the next woman."

"My, oh, my," Arnold said, looking quite amazed. "In a way, that's real comforting. But, if I was a young prince or king, I still wouldn't know how to act around Lady Caroline. And I don't see how you know either."

"I don't," Longarm admitted. "I just try to be myself and let the chips fall where they may."

"I doubt that they'll fall anyplace," Arnold said. "That Mrs. Addie is worse'n a bulldog for watchin' Lady Caroline. She'll sniff out your worst intentions."

"She already has," Longarm said. "But I'm still going

to do my best to get around her."

"Good luck!"

"Thanks," Longarm said, grabbing his traveling bags and saddlebags, "because I'll need it."

After he left the train station and headed into the booming rail and ranching town of Cheyenne, Longarm resisted the temptation to go to the Winston House and ask to see Caroline. He figured that acting too aggressively might scare her off, and it would certainly trigger the displeasure of Mrs. Addie. So Longarm rented a modest room at the new, two-story Teton Hotel. Later, he enjoyed a quiet supper and went out to find a little entertainment in the form of a low-stakes card game or just some friendly conversation.

Normally, Longarm would have visited the old and venerable Elkhorn Saloon, where he knew the bartenders and most of the regulars. Tonight, however, he reminded himself that he was supposed to be looking and acting like a businessman. So instead, Longarm decided to try a few new places, the kind that catered to a wealthier class of visitor. A place like the Rutherford Inn, where well-heeled travelers felt welcome and safe from the rowdier types that preyed on them at the railroad towns.

When Longarm went inside the Rutherford, he removed his hat because everyone else had done so, and there was a nicely dressed man who offered to take not only his new Stetson, but also his coat.

"I'll wear the coat," Longarm said. "Just point me in the direction of the bar."

"The *saloon* is off to your right, restaurant to the left. Will you be dining alone?"

"I won't be dining at all," Longarm said. "I'm just

looking to enjoy a few drinks and a some congenial company."

"Very good," the man said formally. "I'm sure that you will find our saloon to your liking."

"As long as they serve good whiskey for under four bits a shot, I'll get along fine."

The man's expression changed. "I'm afraid that the drinks are a little bit steeper than that."

"How steep?"

"One dollar, I believe, is the minimum."

"Holy cow! I can buy a bottle and . . ." Longarm remembered himself and clamped his mouth shut before he walked on into the saloon. He guessed he could buy a round or two and then he'd call it a night.

The saloon was dim and only half full, with about twenty men, all wearing suits, starched white shirts, ties, and collars. Longarm was aware that heads turned when he sauntered across to the bar and ordered a whiskey. He was big and rugged enough that men as well as woman appraised him with admiration.

"Good evening, sir," the bartender said with a slight but definite bow. "How can I serve you this evening?"

Longarm was impressed. No bartender he'd ever seen had been this solicitous. "Well," he mused, as if he hadn't already decided, "I believe I'll have one of your best whiskeys."

"What brand, sir?"

Longarm was stumped. He normally bought whatever the house brand was unless it was Old Wild Weasel, a particularly venomous brew. Now, Longarm scanned the back bar and said, "I'll take some Mountain Nectar."

"Good choice, but it's brandy, sir, not whiskey."

"Oh, yeah, sure. How about that one," Longarm said,

pointing to a bottle of Kentucky Horse.

The bartender found the handsome bottle and uncorked it. "You've excellent taste."

"Thank you," Longarm said, leaning into the bar and thinking he might actually buy a good Cuban cigar.

The bartender poured him three full fingers and said, "Be three dollars, sir."

"Three dollars!"

The bartender stiffened with surprise. "Sir? Is there something wrong?"

"Yeah, two dollars wrong. I'm not going to be skinned. Why, three dollars ought to buy the whole damned bottle."

"Not at the price it costs us."

"Well," Longarm said indignantly, "three dollars for one drink is robbery. I'm getting out of here while I still have the suit on my back."

"As you wish," the bartender said with cool contempt. "It appears that you wandered into the wrong kind of establishment, eh?"

Longarm did not ignore this callous insult. His hand shot out and he grabbed the bartender by the front of his starched shirt. Longarm dragged him up on his toes and hissed, "You get smart with me, I'll jam that Kentucky Horse down your throat, bottom end first. Do you understand me?"

The bartender's cockiness turned to fear. "Yes, sir!"

Longarm let the man go. He had no patience with this type, and when Longarm turned to see everyone staring at him as if he were a coyote in a hen house, Longarm knew that this just wasn't his kind of drinking place. Longarm wished he had the money to make some outrageously extravagant gesture, like buying rounds of

Kentucky Horse for the whole bunch, but that would have been a foolish gesture.

Instead, Longarm bulled his way outside into the fresh night air and found a little hole-in-the-wall bar named Stetson's that catered to a working class of person like himself. They stared at him in his fancy clothes, but they let him alone, and when the bartender brought Longarm a bottle and a glass he said, "Be two bits a glass, two dollars for the bottle."

"I'll take the bottle," Longarm said, noticing that it was a familiar brand of whiskey.

After a few minutes, the other patrons lost interest in Longarm, and he wandered over to an empty table and seated himself with his back to the wall. He enjoyed watching men, and figured it was good practice to study their habits and to try to fathom their minds.

There were about a dozen customers at the bar and three or four card tables with players. Longarm considered joining them, but the idea of gambling held no appeal. What he really wanted to do was to pay a visit to Caroline. But that would be a mistake, so he'd nip at his bottle for an hour or so and then he'd be off to bed.

At least, that was the plan until a couple of loud and drunken men came stomping into the bar with a pair of girls hanging on their arms.

"Lordy, lordy!" the bigger of the men crowed. "Hey, everybody, over at the Black Jack Saloon I just ran a full house into a hundred-dollar pot and I'm ready to howl! Drinks on the house for everyone!"

The room burst into cheers and men drained their glasses and stampeded to the bar.

"Hey," the prettiest of the two young women said as

she glanced over and saw that Longarm wasn't hurrying over to join the others, "come on!"

"No, thanks," Longarm said. "I've got my own bottle and I'm just fine."

The smaller of the two celebrants overheard Longarm and said, "It's bad manners not to accept drinks on the house when they're offered. Everyone knows that."

"Well, I don't," Longarm replied, "so just go ahead and enjoy your friend's good fortune and leave me be."

"You hear that, Big J?" the smaller man said, loud enough for everyone to hear. "You just been insulted."

Big J was the man buying drinks on the house. He turned and waved Longarm over. When Longarm shook his head, Big J stomped over to his table. "I'm buyin', you're drinkin'. It's that simple."

Longarm heard the threat and chose to ignore it. "I heard you but, as you can see, I have a half bottle left of my own, so save your money."

Big J's face darkened. The girl he'd had his arm around didn't want trouble. "Just let him along, Big J. The stranger ain't harming no one."

"He's insulting me."

"No, he isn't! He's just a dude that don't know our ways."

"Are you a dude?" Big J asked, planting his huge hands on the table in front of Longarm and speaking right into his face.

"Nope," Longarm said, "but I am a man that doesn't like to be pushed. So back off and enjoy your good fortune while I enjoy my peace."

Big J didn't take advice very well. "You sonofabitch in your fancy suit and tie, I ought to—"

Longarm had picked up his bottle as if to pour a drink,

but instead brought it up hard against Big J's head. The man dropped like a stone.

"You bastard!" Big J's friend screamed, going for his six-gun.

Longarm's Colt came up first and he fired, sending a slug into the man's upper arm.

"You broke my arm!" he cried, gun spilling from his hand onto the floor.

"You're damned lucky just to be alive," Longarm said as he collected the man's fallen weapon. "I had every right to kill you."

Longarm stepped around Big J, who had collapsed to his knees cursing and raving. When Longarm neared the end of the bar three railroad workers tried to block his path, but Longarm stopped before them and said, "I'm in no mood for interference, so I'd advise you boys to step aside."

"And if we don't?" one of them challenged drunkenly.

Longarm still held his gun in one hand and his bottle in the other. Leveling the gun, he stared into the man's eyes and growled, "Those two behind me are just wounded and they'll recover. But if you don't move now, you just might not be so lucky."

The man's nerve broke and he stumbled aside. The others quickly followed. Longarm passed through the door thinking that he should have gone straight back to his hotel room and gone to bed. He was nearing the hotel when he heard the rapid pounding of footsteps behind him. Longarm turned to see Big J's young lady companion hurrying up to him. She was crying and there was a smear of blood on her swollen lower lip.

"What happened?" Longarm asked.

"Big J punched me! For no damned reason, he just hauled back and hit me in the face."

"Well," Longarm said, dragging out his handkerchief, "when you wallow with hogs, you're bound to get dirty."

"Can I have a drink?" she asked, dabbing her handkerchief to her lip.

"Sure." Longarm gave her the bottle. "Help yourself."

"You're a real gentleman," she said, upending the bottle and drinking like a draft horse.

"Whoa!" Longarm said. "I might want a little nightcap up in my room."

"Where are you staying?"

"Why do you ask?"

"Well, I thought me and Big J were going to celebrate, but now . . ."

"I'm a little tired," Longarm hedged.

She was persistent and thirsty. "Strangers in Cheyenne shouldn't drink alone."

"Is that right?"

They were standing near one of the city's new street lamps, and he thought she looked quite pretty, even with teary eyes and a puffy lip. "How old are you?"

"Twenty. How old are you?"

"Older."

"You got a handsome face."

"Thanks. My boss said I don't look so good."

"Your boss is probably jealous," she told him. "I think you're a lot handsomer than Big J, that ornery sonofabitch."

"Yeah, but he has a hundred dollars, which is a lot more money than I have to spend in a saloon on whiskey and pretty women like you."

The girl loved flattery and smiled. "You dress nice and I'll bet you have lots of money."

"You bet wrong," Longarm told her.

"I don't care," she said after a minute. "I need a few drinks and it'd be nice to talk to an honorable man for a change."

Longarm glanced up at his second-story hotel room window. It was dark and the night was going to be cold. "Maybe you could come up and we could share the rest of this bottle."

She brightened. "My name is Irma. What's yours?"

"Custis."

"Nice name. Nice clothes. Nice body."

"Come on, Irma," he said, slipping his arm around the girl's slender waist. "Let's go to bed."

She pulled back, but not hard. "But what about the drinking and talking?"

"We can do that too, later."

Irma giggled. She took his bottle and had another pull, and then she wiped her lip again with his ruined handkerchief. "All right," she said, "first we screw, then we get acquainted, all right?"

"That'll be fine, Irma."

Longarm found that he wasn't as tired as he had thought. The minute Irma undressed and slipped into bed, he was on her like an animal. She had nice, lush breasts, and he licked them until the nipples stood up like dark little peaks. Very soon she took his stiff rod and guided it into her moist honeypot, and then wrapped her powerful thighs around his hips.

"Nice, real nice," she moaned as Longarm began to thrust into her hot wetness.

Longarm didn't hurry himself. He hadn't had a woman in several weeks, and Irma was skilled enough to know how to stretch a man to the breaking point, then ease back and leave his body tingling. Longarm was able to handle that about three times before fire flowed through his big rod and into Irma's body, causing her to buck and squeal when her passion exploded like a Chinese rocket.

"We were really good together, Custis," she panted when he rolled off her and reached for the whiskey. "You've been with a lot of women, haven't you."

"I guess."

"What do you do?"

He decided to tell her the truth. "I'm a United States marshal."

Irma sat bolt upright. "No!"

"It's the truth," he said. "I could climb out of this bed and show you my badge."

"Holy shit!" she exclaimed. "I never gave to no lawman before."

Longarm offered her the bottle. "Have a drink, honey. The world is just full of surprises, and worse things could happen to a girl like you."

Irma took the bottle and drank, but her eyes never left Longarm's face, and when she had her fill of the whiskey, she said, "Honest to Pete? You're a federal lawman?"

"That's right."

"But how come you're dressed up so fancy?"

"It's a long, long story, Irma, and one that I really can't tell."

"Are you staying in Cheyenne for a while? I wouldn't mind getting a lot more of you, Marshal."

He laughed. "No, I'm afraid that I'm boarding the westbound train first thing tomorrow morning."

Her face dropped. "I'm sorry to hear that. Big J might try to beat me up again. I don't suppose you'd like to buy me a ticket west? We could travel together and we could screw day and night. I'd make it worth your while, I swear that I would!"

"I believe you," Longarm said, "but I just can't do that. I'm traveling on the taxpayers' tab. They wouldn't like it one bit if I paid your way."

"Screw 'em."

"You can try it. I can't."

"Well, can you at least buy me a ticket over to Laramie? If Big J catches me tomorrow, I'd get a hell of a beating."

"How much is a ticket to Laramie?"

"Six dollars."

"Sure," Longarm said. "I'll give you six dollars."

"Thanks!"

"Let's not talk anymore," he said, setting the bottle down on his bedside table and taking Irma into his arms.

"Maybe we can screw a little on the way over the Laramies," she said.

"I don't think so."

"Why?"

Longarm thought of the English women, and could well imagine how unfavorably they would view a prostitute like Irma.

"I just don't think that would work," he said.

"You mean it wouldn't look right to some people on that train that you want to impress."

Longarm was struck by her perceptiveness, and even

a little embarrassed. "Yeah," he confessed, "but then, I guess I've never given much thought to how other people judge me, so why start now."

"Good!" Irma looked happy again. "Can you find us a place to do it?"

"It depends on how big a private traveling compartment they give me this time," he told her. "The one I had up from Denver wasn't big enough for a pair of cats to couple."

"I hope you get a bigger one this time," she said, reaching for his manhood. "I'll bet that we can do it about a dozen times before we get over those tall mountains."

Longarm knew that was ridiculous, but there was no reason not to at least try.

41

Chapter 4

The westbound Union Pacific left precisely at eight-ten in the morning, and fortunately for Longarm, it was forty minutes late pulling into Cheyenne. He was really dragging when he hauled his luggage as well as Irma's up to the train and shoved his ticket at the conductor, who was standing on the station platform.

"First class, Marshal?" the conductor asked, eyebrows raised in doubt.

"That's right!" Longarm said, annoyed by the question. "Pete, is there something wrong with my ticket?"

The conductor studied it closely. "No, it's a first-class ticket all right. I just didn't think that the government was in the habit of providing marshals with such luxury. What happened, Longarm, did you get a big promotion or save our president's life?"

"No on both counts," Longarm said. "Which compartment have I been assigned?"

The conductor looked at his clipboard. "You're in . . ." He didn't finish, but the corners of his mouth turned up in a grin. "I'm afraid I spoke too soon about that first-class ticket."

"What's that supposed to mean?" Longarm asked, suddenly expecting the worst.

"It means you have been assigned the sweatbox."

"The what?"

"It's next to the furnace," the conductor explained. "Old ladies sometimes enjoy it, but the heat radiates right through the wall and it becomes damned hot."

Longarm bit back an oath. "I want something else."

"I'm sorry, Marshal. All the other first-class compartments have been booked up for weeks. Number three is always the last to go because it gets so danged hot inside."

Longarm was incensed. "Well, why don't they just insulate the wall between number three and the furnace?"

"If they tried to do it with wood, it most likely would catch fire. If they do it with metal, which they have, the metal just conducts the heat like a frying pan on a stove."

"Surely it must have a window I can open to at least keep the temperature bearable."

"Nope. You see, number three was originally a storage room. But they made it into a sleeping compartment."

Pete frowned. "I'm sure that your department must have known about this compartment and took it because of the discount."

"Discount?" Longarm's jaw dropped.

"Why, sure! We had so many complaints over number three that they dropped the first-class fare to just ten dollars over the price of a second-class ticket."

"I'll kill Billy," Longarm vowed passionately.

"Marshal, before you get too upset, remember that you do get to eat your meals in the Hotel Express dining car,

43

and that does cost an extra four dollars a day."

The conductor reached for another passenger's ticket. "Really, Marshal, it's hot in number three, but you can hang out in the parlor car and you'll still eat like a king."

Only slightly mollified, Longarm went over to Irma and picked up her bags. She said, "You don't look very happy. Is there a problem?"

"I'll tell you about it later," he growled. "Let's get you on board and get you a seat in second class, and then you can come down and join me in number three."

"Number three?" Irma wrinkled her cute little nose. "I think I've heard about that compartment. Isn't it called—"

"Yeah, the sweatbox."

"Great," she said. "We can work off all the wonderful food we'll eat in the dining car."

"I'm afraid that you're not going to be allowed to join me in the first-class dining car. It's against the rules."

Irma wasn't pleased.

"We'll be in Laramie in less than four hours," Longarm said, wanting to console her.

"All right." Irma sighed, slipped her arm through his, and forced a bloated smile because of her puffy lip. "Let's board and not let anything spoil our short time together."

As they walked back over to the boarding steps, the conductor took Irma's ticket and said, "Second class goes right toward the rear, first class left toward the front."

"Yeah, sure," Longarm muttered.

"What happened to your lip, young lady?" Pete asked as he punched Irma's ticket and returned it to her. "Did this big fella do that?"

It was meant as a joke, but neither Longarm nor Irma so much as cracked a smile.

"Next," Pete said as he looked past them.

"Thank you," said the pretty and familiar female voice.

Longarm slowly turned around, and there were Lady Caroline and Mrs. Addie waiting behind him.

"Good morning, Mr. Long." Caroline directed her perfect smile at Irma. "I don't believe we've been introduced."

"My name is Irma. Who are you?"

"I'm Caroline."

"*Lady* Caroline," Mrs. Addie corrected. "And do you have a last name, Irma?"

"Sure."

"And it is?"

"Stanton. Irma Eloise Stanton."

"I am Mrs. Addie. That lip does look pretty swollen. Have you consulted a doctor?"

"Naw. It'll be all right. Hurts when Custis kisses me too hard, but he's worth the pain, aren't cha."

Longarm was mercifully spared further embarrassment because the locomotive engineer blasted his steam whistle and Pete called, "All aboard!"

"I hope we have a chance to get to know each other better," Lady Caroline said to Irma with genuine warmth. "I'm sure that you are a very fascinating person."

"Uh," Longarm stammered, "that won't be possible, I'm afraid."

"Why not?"

"Irma gets off at Laramie."

"I'd like to go all the way to Sacramento, though," Irma said quickly. "I never been to California, but I hear it's pretty and always warm."

"We're going to Sacramento," Caroline said sweetly, "It would be nice if you could too."

Irma shrugged even as Longarm grabbed her arm and practically threw her onto the train. "No money for a ticket that far."

"Custis?" Caroline asked, looking concerned. "Is that poor girl all right?"

"Sure," he replied. "She's just . . . tired."

"Oh." Caroline looked relieved. "The girl probably just needs a nap."

"Yes," Longarm said as he excused himself and clambered into the train to direct Irma toward the second-class coach while he sought out his first-class accommodations.

A few minutes later, when Longarm found compartment number three and opened the door, the heat inside struck him in the face like the heat off a blacksmith's forge.

"Sonofabitch!" he swore. "It must be a hundred and ten in here! Pete!"

But the conductor was nowhere to be seen. Longarm felt the train lurch forward. He hesitated, then peeled off his coat and removed his tie before he stepped back inside, sweat running from every pore in his body. At least, Longarm rationalized, the compartment was spacious and the bed was just wide and long enough to accommodate himself and sweet, passionate Irma.

Longarm kicked off his boots, coat, and shirt, then flopped down on the bed with mounting anticipation. "Where is that girl?" he asked himself out loud.

Longarm lay sweating and waiting for about half an hour before there was a knock on his compartment door. "Custis?"

46

"Come on in!"

Irma opened the door and her eyes widened. "Whew! It's *really* hot in here!"

"It's warm, all right. But bearable. Why don't you come inside and close the door?"

"I can't."

He sat up. "What does that mean?"

"Lady Caroline had invited me to join her."

"What!"

"Custis, I've never had the . . . the privilege of meeting royalty before and I'm sure I won't ever again. I want to talk to her."

Longarm reached out and practically dragged Irma into his compartment. He closed the door behind her and said, "Listen, you won't have a thing to say to that woman."

"What makes you so damned sure of that?"

"I just know," Longarm said.

"Well, she really sounded as if she wanted to talk to me. I'll tell her the truth. I think she wants to meet a real frontier woman."

"Which you are not."

"Am too!" Irma pulled away from Longarm. "You just want me to stay here so we can sweat and hump ourselves to a frazzle. Lady Caroline is interested in my *mind*."

"Oh, for crying out loud!" Longarm groaned. "I thought we were going to make love a dozen times going over the Laramie Mountains."

"That's before I met a real princess."

"She's no princess!"

Irma's eyes flashed with anger, and sweat was beading on her upper lip, which Longarm found very sensual.

He wanted her, and he'd paid for her ticket to Laramie and saved her from a beating, but he was too proud and too much the gentleman to remind her of these things.

"You want to go visit Lady Caroline, then you go right on ahead," Longarm snapped.

"I will!"

And she did.

Longarm was furious. This was supposed to be a restful and luxurious trip out to Reno and it was turning into a misery. He found his handkerchief and mopped his brow, feeling salty sweat burn his eyes. He was going to *lose* weight, not gain it after three days in this miserable sweatbox.

Longarm must have dozed for a couple of hours, because he was suddenly awakened by a knock on his door. "Custis?"

"Go away, Irma. Have some tea and crumpets with the blue bloods."

"You want to come and join us?"

"No."

"Are you angry at me?"

"Yep."

"Can I please come in?"

He almost said no a second time, but good sense saved him. "All right," he said, "come in."

Irma came into the compartment, looked at him, and said, "You're all wet."

"Yeah."

"You need towels to dry off with."

"I need more than towels."

Irma began to unbutton her blouse. "I can see that."

"What are you doing?"

"You know."

"What about Lady Caroline?"

"I really like her, but Mrs. Addie is a pill. She doesn't like me very much. So I excused myself and came to say good-bye."

Longarm felt like a heel, but what was a man to do when a girl as pretty and passionate as Irma was already half undressed.

"We got an hour or two still before we get to Laramie," she said with a coy smile. "But we're going to be so wet and slick that we'll probably keep sliding over the edge of that skinny little berth and falling on the floor. If I'm on the bottom and you're big and hard inside me, I could get hurt."

"I promise that won't happen," he said.

Irma was reassured enough to smile. "You're a very nice man, Marshal Long. I sure wish I was traveling all the way to Reno with you."

"Well, I do too," he heard himself say, and realized that he meant it. "I think it would be best all the way around if we parted company in Laramie."

She unbuttoned his pants and found his manhood. "Custis, I really am dead broke. Do you suppose I could borrow ten or twenty dollars?"

He could not refuse her. "Yeah."

Irma beamed. "You *are* a nice man!"

"Just peel off those panties and quit talking so much, all right?"

"Whatever you say."

Longarm kicked off his pants, and Irma her panties. Her big breasts were already glistening with sweat, and he could hardly wait to lick them dry. Irma climbed on

49

top of him, and when she eased down on his thick root, she sighed.

"Talk can get old after a little while, Custis, even with a princess."

"I guess it can," he said, pulling her breasts down to his hungry mouth and thrusting upward with his rod until she squirmed and moaned with pleasure. "Sometimes, it's better just to screw."

"I agree."

Their sweaty bodies made loud sucking sounds as they slammed in and out of each other and the train struggled over the mountains toward Laramie.

Much later, when the train actually did pull into Laramie, Longarm was having too good a time to let Irma go.

"What would you think if I extended your ticket on to Rock Springs?"

"Anything. Anyplace. Just don't stop doing this to me, Custis!"

"Maybe you'd even like Elko better," Longarm gasped.

"Why not Reno?" she panted.

As Longarm grew ready to spew his hot seed into Irma, he decided that Reno would be just fine.

Chapter 5

Longarm considered himself a patient and even forgiving man, but after two days of roasting in his traveling compartment, he knew that something drastic had to be done soon. Irma and Lady Caroline had struck up a peculiar friendship that had no common basis as far as Longarm could tell other than they were both young and very attractive women.

The pair of unlikely new friends now spent most of their days together, talking about all matter of things relating to England, the American frontier, and such mundane things as the price of dresses and shoes. Longarm was completely bored, and so he found himself spending more and more time in the parlor car, and also in the second-class traveling coach where an ordinary fella could scare up some good, down-to-earth talk and an honest low-stakes poker game that never really ended.

In this way, Longarm had managed to spend all but his nights away from the "sweatbox" compartment number three. At night, however, he and Irma would make furious love despite being bathed in perspiration.

"You can't be serious," Irma said one hot night as their train chugged across the flat, broken sagebrush of northern Utah. "If you wreck the furnace, all the other first-class compartments will get very cold at night."

"I realize that," Longarm said. "And I've even pleaded with the porter to lower the temperature, but he refused. He said he'd be fired if he allowed the heat to drop and the other first-class passengers started complaining."

"Well," Irma said, "you can't just destroy the furnace."

"That's exactly what I'm going to do," Longarm vowed.

"But you're an officer of the law!"

"I'm a man who is at his wit's end," Longarm replied. "I need to fix that damned furnace so that it can't be repaired until this train reaches Sacramento."

"How on earth are you going to do that?"

"I've been giving it some thought," Longarm replied. "In fact, I've been giving it a *lot* of thought."

"And?"

"I'm going to riddle the boiler and put it permanently out of commission."

"You'll be scalded alive," Irma said. "I think it would be much safer just to destroy a section of the heating duct."

"They could make a replacement too easily," Longarm said with a shake of his head. "After all, the railroad has repair shops all along the line."

"If they can repair the duct, they can repair the boiler itself."

"Sure they can," Longarm said, "but we're running behind schedule and a major repair will have to wait until the train reaches Sacramento. There are three big repair shops on this line. Sacramento, Cheyenne, and Omaha. They'd have to go on to Sacramento."

Irma sighed and continued to dress. "Well," she said, "you do what you have to do. I'm going to go join Caroline for supper. Do you want to come along?"

"Maybe later."

"All right," Irma said, mopping her face and arms dry before leaving their overheated compartment.

As soon as she was gone, Longarm consulted his pocket watch. The porter in charge of stoking the furnace was a creature of habit whose work routine did not vary.

Exactly five minutes later, Longarm heard the bang of the coal furnace door being slammed open. Then he heard the porter shoveling coal. Longarm counted the shovelfuls and there were exactly twenty. In about thirty minutes, the furnace would be roaring hot, the boiler would be belching steam, and the temperature in Longarm's compartment would be over one hundred degrees.

When the furnace door banged shut again, Longarm came to his feet and opened his door. He peered up and down the aisle and, seeing that it was empty, tiptoed around to the furnace, which was already popping and would soon exhibit a cherry-red glow.

Reaching into his pants pockets, Longarm retrieved a dozen .44-caliber bullets. Taking a deep breath, he found the heavy pair of cowhide leather gloves that the porter used to open the furnace door. Longarm put one on his left hand and unlatched the furnace door.

When he swung the heavy, cast-iron door open, the blast of fire was so intense that Longarm recoiled and was certain that his face was scorched and that his mustache, eyebrows, and hair were singed and would, therefore, mark him as the guilty party in this ridiculous affair.

"Here goes," he said, tossing in a handful of his gun's .44-caliber cartridges. He slammed the door, latched it tight, ducked around the corner, and then hurried down the aisle toward second class. He had not gone more than fifteen feet when the first cartridge exploded.

The effect was more that Longarm could have possibly imagined. The explosions were akin to cannon fire, and so thunderous that the very walls of the coach shook. They came so rapidly that they blended into a long but united clap of rolling thunder.

"Hey," a passenger shouted, bursting in from the second-class coach and starting toward the furnace. "What's going on?"

"Beats me," Longarm said, blocking the man's progress, "but it sounds like a gunfight and you'd better go back to your seat."

The passenger made a quick and complete change of direction. Longarm followed him out.

"There must be a gunfight of some sort going on in the first-class sleeping coach!" another passenger shouted as they entered the second-class coach.

"I'll check it out," Longarm shouted, wheeling back around as the sound of his bullets finally died. To make it look convincing, Longarm dragged his Colt from its holster and marched back into the first-class coach. He could already smell smoke and steam, and was suddenly worried that an unwitting passenger might inhale the noxious and potentially fatal fumes.

Holstering his six-gun, Longarm plunged ahead. When he reached the end of the car he saw that the furnace, boiler, and even chimney were completely destroyed. Steam was gushing out of the boiler and drenching the furnace, causing the cast iron to pop and bang. Boiling water flooded across the floor, and the small furnace area was the scene of complete chaos as two porters dashed about trying to figure out exactly what to do.

"Anything I can do to help?" Longarm asked, innocent as a choirboy.

"No," the porter shouted in anger. "Marshal, I expect you're the one that caused this . . . this 'accident'!"

Longarm pivoted around on his heels and yelled to the curious men who had followed him in from the second-class coach. "The situation is under control now. Everyone back out of here so that the porters can clean up."

"Well, what the hell happened?" a man yelled. "Did anyone even get shot?"

"Nope," Longarm said. "Steam heater exploded. Just a minor inconvenience for us first-class passengers. It isn't a big deal."

"There ought to be better maintenance on this equipment," another man grumped. "Why, if one of us passengers had of been standing beside that furnace when she blew, we'd probably be dead!"

"Probably," Longarm agreed. "Is anybody up for a game of poker?"

Several men were.

"Then let's get started."

Longarm knew that the whole train crew would soon suspect that he was the culprit. The truth of the matter was that Longarm simply did not care. No doubt the Union Pacific would eventually repair their first-class coach's heating apparatus, and compartment number three would again be the infamous sweatbox. Longarm

55

didn't care as long as he could finally be comfortable in the meantime.

That night it actually got chilly in the first-class coach, and the next morning Mrs. Addie complained bitterly about the temperature, but no one paid her a good deal of attention. Longarm and Irma had made cool love and slept dry for the first time since leaving Cheyenne.

When the train pulled into Elko, Nevada, Longarm escorted Lady Caroline, Mrs. Addie, and Irma into town to do some shopping and sightseeing during the scheduled two-hour layover. Having been in this hell-on-wheels rail town many times, Longarm knew the shops that they would want to visit, and had decided that he would devote himself to their needs. After all, this would be the last stopover until they all parted company in Reno.

"Elko is one of my favorite holdovers along this run," Longarm said as they strolled along the boardwalk. "Unlike some of the railroad towns, this one has a church, a school, and an air of civility. It also depends a lot less on the railroad for its existence."

"Why is that?" Caroline asked.

"Because this is such excellent cattle and sheep country," Longarm explained. "Some of the biggest and most successful ranching operations in the West can be found in this country. Over to the southeast are the Ruby Mountains, and they're tall, cool, and beautiful. There are a lot of wild mustangs in this part of Nevada."

"Perhaps we should stay over for a few days," Caroline said, looking at Mrs. Addie.

"No," she said, "I don't think that would be such a good idea. What is Reno like, Mr. Long?"

"It's bigger and will have more comforts for you ladies," he told them. "Also, there are a lot of wild

56

horse herds in the surrounding country."

"Then I definitely think we should go on," Mrs. Addie said, her brow furrowed with concern. "But of course, that is your decision to make, Lady Caroline."

"Perhaps you are right," Caroline said, "although I can almost feel the excitement in this town."

"It's pretty wild and wooly here on Saturday night," Longarm told them. "But I think that it would be more enjoyable for you to stop over in Reno. There are also a lot more stores, and you might even want to take a side trip up to the nearby Comstock Lode. It's in a steep financial decline, the ore having run out in most of the big mines like the Belcher and the Ophir, but Piper's Opera House, saloons like the Bucket of Blood and the Delta Queen, as well as some of the old mansions and the beautiful St. Mary of the Mountains Church are sights that you will never forget."

"Then let's go on," Caroline said. She looked to Irma. "You are going on, aren't you?"

"Yes," she said, smiling sweetly at Longarm. "I have found a gentleman whose kindness and generosity allow me to continue on to Reno."

Longarm's cheeks blushed and he said, "Ladies, I'm going to go have a drink and play a few rounds of cards. Our two-hour layover ought to be plenty of time for you to browse the shops and stores."

A rough-looking cowboy passed them slowly, staring boldly at Caroline and Irma. Mrs. Addie stiffened with indignation. "Are you sure that it's safe?"

"Yes," Longarm told them. "And if you have any trouble, I'll be at the Elko Saloon, just a few doors up on this side of the street. All you have to do is sing out and I'll come running."

"I'll take care of them," Irma said. "If nothing else, I know how to handle men."

This candid remark surprised Longarm, and told him that Irma must have confessed her past sins in some detail to these two English ladies. And Longarm guessed that was all for the best, that probably Irma had been accepted because of her honesty.

"Fair enough," Longarm said, tipping his hat to the ladies and heading off to find a cigar, a whiskey, and some fresh conversation.

The Elko Saloon was a cowboy hangout. The walls had the many local cattle outfits' brands burned into them. There were old, broken saddles slung over the rafters and covered with dust and cobwebs, and a couple of longhorn steer heads decorated the walls with their enormous spans of black-tipped horns. One of the longhorns had the stump of a cigar stuffed between its jaws. In addition, there were several Indian lances and rusty trade rifles nailed to the walls, trophies of an earlier, far more dangerous era.

"Well, well!" the bartender called. "If it isn't Deputy Marshal Custis Long. And ain't you the fancy one in that new suit, hat, and cowboy boots! What happened? Did you start collecting your own rewards?"

Several of the cowboys broke into easy laughter, and even Longarm had to grin. "How ya doin', Jake? Good to see you again."

"And you," Jake said, looking genuinely pleased. "You know it's always a pleasure to see you come through my door. First drink is on me. What'll you have?"

"I'll have the usual snake poison," Longarm said, knowing that the house brand of whiskey was pretty good and not watered down the way it often was in the rail town saloons.

Jake filled him a glass and then filled one for himself. He was a slope-shouldered man in his late forties, nearly bald but with a thick, luxurious mat of beard.

"To good health and friends," Jake said, raising his glass in salute.

Longarm nodded and raised his own glass. The whiskey went down smooth and he emptied his glass, smacked his lips, and said, "You always did carry good liquor, Jake. How are things in Elko these days?"

"Things are good. Cattle prices are down a little, but they'll come back up. The railroad is planning to replace some trestles just east of us, and they'll have to bring in about a hundred section hands and builders this month. That will help all of us businessmen."

"It will," Longarm agreed. "Are the mustangers still working the Ruby Mountains and bringing in a lot of wild horses?"

"There's still a few left," Jake said, "but not near as many as a couple years back. What we have now are the Indians who have pretty much taken that business over. They'll stay out in the brush and are happy just to catch a dozen mustangs all summer. They break 'em to ride and then sell 'em to the army and to the locals. What they can't sell because they're runts or cripples will be sold to the meat buyers who ship them east for dog food. I hear tell that the folks in Europe eat horsemeat like it was a delicacy."

"I've also heard that," Longarm admitted. "But I sure can't imagine a man eating a horse unless he was starving."

"The Apache like horses and mules better than cattle."

"Yeah," Longarm said, "but the Apache have never been known as being picky about anything."

Longarm ordered a second round of drinks for himself and Jake. They sipped this round and talked about things of general interest, mostly the weather and the politics of the state of Nevada and nearby Utah.

"I might sell out and move over to California one of these days," Jake confessed. "If I can find a buyer with enough cash money."

"Why would you want to do a thing like that?" Longarm asked. "You have a fine reputation and a nice little business."

"Sure it is, but about once a month we have a real bad brawl in here. Cowboys get liquored up and start to raise hell. They bust the place up."

"Don't you make 'em pay for the damages?"

"I try to, but they're always broke. We haul them off to court, but they choose jail rather than pay fines. I'm the one left holding the empty bag, and that can be expensive. And then too, one of these times I just might catch a stray bullet."

"That can happen," Longarm said. "What about Marshal Todd? Doesn't he keep a lid on the troublemakers?"

"Oh, he tries," Jake said. "On Saturday nights he comes around, and he'll haul the worst of 'em out of the saloons and lock them in that little rock house jail. But as soon as he's made his rounds, the bad apples left behind just get rowdy all over again. And Marshal Todd is no spring chicken. He goes to bed at nine o'clock every night, and it better be an emergency before you dare to roust him out."

"He needs to hang it up and retire. I like Todd, but he must be what? Mid-sixties?"

60

"Seventy-three," Jake said. "Mike Todd was a real town tamer in his younger days, but they are long past. I hear he cleaned up Abilene so fast that the bad ones were bailin' out of there like ticks off a dying dog. He went over to Bodie, California, and damned if he didn't do the same thing there. He's tough, but too damned old."

Longarm had to agree. It was amazing that Todd was still alive considering that he was constantly being forced to arrest men young enough to be his grandsons. Todd was a veteran and plenty careful. He knew all the tricks and never bullied, blustered, or forced men to violence. But still, men did get liquored up and crazy, and Mike Todd was too damned old and slow to brace them and expect to come out a winner.

Longarm had another drink, and then he played a few hands of poker with a couple of cowboys. From them, he learned that the rains had been good in the spring and the grass had been better than it had been in years.

"If we have another couple of good years," one cowboy said with a slow grin, "we might even be able to start feedin' ourselves and our poor horses."

Longarm chuckled. "You boys look well enough fed to me."

"And you look a little lean," the cowboy said. "What's the matter, the government been cuttin' your wages?"

"Nope, they've been running me too damned hard."

Longarm was about to say more when he heard a cry and suddenly Lady Caroline burst breathlessly through the doorway. "Marshal, come quick!"

Longarm bolted out of his chair. "What's wrong?"

"It's Irma. A couple of men are accosting her!"

Longarm wasn't exactly sure what Caroline meant by the term "accosting," but he figured it meant something like giving Irma a bad time. In three strides, he was out the doorway and marching up the boardwalk.

Irma was fighting with a couple of big men who looked to be trying to drag her into an alley. Mrs. Addie was trying to help, but even as Longarm watched, one of the bullies slapped her so hard the poor old woman struck a hitching rail and crumpled to her knees.

"Hey!" Longarm shouted, bursting into a run. "Let go of that woman!"

When they saw Longarm, the two men released Irma and went for their six-guns. There was no hesitation on their parts and Longarm, coming on in full stride, was caught by surprise. He stabbed for his own six-gun as he skidded to a halt, but lost his footing and fell hard.

The two men opened fire, and Longarm rolled in behind a water trough. Cussing at his own helplessness, he dragged his gun out even as slugs sprayed wood and water. He raised his head and damn if one of the big sonofabitches didn't drill his new Stetson through the crown and send it flying.

Longarm cocked back the hammer of his gun and coolly shot both men through the chest even as they started to bolt and run for cover.

It was over just that fast.

"You *killed* them," Caroline said, rushing over to Longarm and biting her knuckles. "You shot them both dead."

"Damn right I did," Longarm said, coming to his feet and marching over to help Mrs. Addie up. "Here," he said to Caroline, "help your friend inside this store and find her a chair. Mrs. Addie looks pretty shaken up."

Longarm went over to Irma. Her dress was torn, her hair was mussed, and now, in addition to that puffy lip, she had the beginnings of a shiner. "Are you all right?"

Irma shook her head and visibly gathered her composure. "Those bastards tried to get fresh with Lady Caroline, can you imagine that!"

"Yes. And I can also well imagine that you stepped in and told them they had no business messing around with royalty. Or something like that. Am I right?"

"I couldn't believe them. They weren't drunk or nothin'. They were just awful!"

"They were quick with their guns," Longarm said. "Quicker than most but a mite too quick on the shoot. They'd have drilled me if they'd been steadier."

Irma hugged Longarm. "I hate men," she whispered. "All of 'em except you, Custis."

Longarm patted her back, and then he was surprised when Irma broke down and began to cry.

Chapter 6

Marshal Mike Todd finished filling out his report, and as Longarm was escorting the three women out of his office, the old lawman said, "Custis?"

"Yeah?"

"Mind if I have a word with you in private?"

"Sure, as long as it's quick. Our train is due to pull out in ten minutes and I have to be on it."

"It'll be brief," Todd promised.

Longarm told the three women to go on to the train station. "I'll catch up with you in a few minutes," he promised.

When the door closed, Longarm turned and said, "What is it, Mike?"

"It's me," the old lawman said. "I'm not able to do the job anymore."

"What do you mean?"

"I mean those two you had to kill weren't strangers to Elko. They'd been here before and raised hell. Never attacked a woman or anything like that, but I knew they were trouble."

"Well, Mike, you don't have to worry about 'em anymore," Longarm said.

"Yeah, I know that," Todd said. "But there will be others just like 'em and I won't be man enough to run 'em off before something like this happens again."

Longarm expelled a deep breath. He liked this man, and had worked with him on a few occasions. Mike Todd was a mite too set in his ways and not very flexible about learning new techniques of law enforcement, but he was brave, forthright, and honest, which made up for all the other shortcomings.

"What are you trying to tell me, Mike?"

"I need to retire," the old man said. "I'm worn plumb out. I'm finished as a lawman and ready for a rocking chair."

"Are you sure?"

"Yep. Custis, if it had of been me out there today instead of you, I'd be dead and those two ornery bastards would be terrorizing that girl and maybe the whole town."

Longarm knew this was probably the truth. And yet, he couldn't openly agree. "Maybe you *should* retire, Mike. It's a tough job."

"It's a younger man's job. A job for a man like you."

"I already have a job."

"Quit it and take my badge," Todd blurted. "I get paid sixty dollars a month and the town has a little house that it lets me use for—"

"Mike," Longarm interrupted, "I just can't do that."

The marshal of Elko clamped his mouth shut and his brow furrowed. Suddenly, the lawman looked even older than his years. "Why not?"

"Because I like my own federal job better," Longarm said, telling him in the most straightforward way possible. "I wouldn't be happy stuck in this cow town. My feet are too itchy, if you know what I mean."

"I do, but there's some awfully nice folks here," Todd countered, "and they support their marshal. Maybe you could even get a raise and—"

"I'm sorry," Longarm said, coming up and placing a hand on Mike's thin shoulder. "But what I'll do is to telegraph my Denver office and let Billy Vail know that you'd like to retire. Maybe someone on our staff would rather be settled than riding stagecoaches and railroads all over the frontier the way I do."

"Would you do that?" Todd asked, looking quite relieved.

"Sure," Longarm promised.

"And . . . and talk to the marshals in Reno, Carson City, and Virginia City. If they seem like good men, tell 'em to write or telegraph me and we can take it on our own from there. They've got to be first-rate, though. I won't leave this town unprotected or at the mercy of someone who isn't."

"I understand. And what about you? Do you have a pension or any savings?"

"I've squirreled a few thousand dollars up and it's gathering interest in the bank. Comes time, I'll either buy the house I'm in now or buy another. I'm a pretty damn good gunsmith, and I know I can pick up ten or fifteen dollars a month repairing firearms. I'll be just fine and dandy."

"Why don't you find some rich old gal to marry," Longarm teased.

"I'm looking for a rich *young* girl to marry," Todd said with a broad smile.

"Aren't we all," Longarm said with amusement, "aren't we all."

"Who is that beautiful woman?"

"Irma?"

"No, the young one that has an English accent."

"She's Lady Caroline."

"What are they doin' out here?"

"Traveling across the West on a train. They're going to stay awhile in Reno, then go on over the Sierras to Sacramento and on to San Francisco."

"Is she as rich as she is pretty?"

Longarm laughed. "Hell, I don't know, Mike. Why don't you ask her?"

"I would if I was you," Todd said. "Damn right I would. I'd be after her like a bird dog after a wounded duck."

"Yeah," Longarm said, "I'm sure that you would be."

He started to say more, but the shriek of the distant steam whistle changed his mind. "So long, Mike. I've got to run."

"Stop by when you come back through," the old lawman said. "We'll have a few snorts and talk about guns and outlaws."

"I'll do that," Longarm promised.

He was already moving down the boardwalk at a run when Todd called, "And don't forget what I asked you!"

"I won't!"

• • •

67

Longarm barely made it onto the train. In fact, it was rolling when he swung on board.

"You're cutting it awfully close, Marshal Long," the conductor said with a frown of disapproval. "But then, I heard about you gunning down those two mean bastards who tried to rape that pretty girl you're traveling with."

"Yeah," Longarm said. "They were bad ones."

"What do you think gets into that kind?"

"I don't know," Longarm said, "and I don't much care. If they break the law, I just arrest or shoot them."

"It's easier and cheaper to shoot that kind," the conductor said.

"I agree."

Longarm went back to his compartment and changed his shirt, which had gotten dirty when he'd had to roll in the street dodging bullets. He was furious about the hole in his new Stetson, but he figured that someone could fix that up without a great deal of trouble. Maybe he could find a gal to sew a little piece of black felt inside so you would hardly notice. He sure wasn't going to throw away a thirty-three-dollar hat because of one little bullet hole.

"Marshal Long?"

Longarm opened the door to see Lady Caroline standing in the aisle. "Well, hello. Can I help you?"

"I'd like to speak to you in private for a moment, if you don't mind."

"No, of course not."

Caroline stepped into his compartment and closed the door behind her. She filled the room with the scent of roses, and Longarm suddenly felt the temperature rising again, just like before he'd wrecked the furnace. He had never been alone with this woman before, and now they

68

were packed into a space small enough that it brought them into physical intimacy.

Mopping his suddenly perspiring brow, Longarm said, "What would you like to talk about?"

Lady Caroline's blue eyes were flecked with gold dust, and Longarm thought he had never seen eyes so large or beautiful.

"I wanted to apologize for how stupid I acted after the shooting."

"Stupid?"

"Yes," she said with a firm nod. "I was shocked almost senseless by the savage violence that took place between you and those two awful men. I reacted badly."

"Have you ever seen men die suddenly before?"

"No, and I hope never to again."

"I feel the same way," he said. "There's nothing good about killing. Every time I've had to shoot and kill, I've felt hollow inside."

"Never victorious or . . . or joyful?"

"Only in the sense that it was the other person who died instead of me. I've always felt it was a tragic waste. Every man I've killed was once an infant in his mother's loving arms. Later a kid with a hoop and stick, laughing and doing all the things that kids do. Then a man, dying in the dust with his blood pumping out of his veins and wondering if there really is a heaven or a hell, or just nothing but an eternal, cold, and absolute blackness."

Caroline took a deep breath. "You are a remarkable man, Mr. Long. I've never met anyone remotely like you."

He forced a smile. "I'm going to take that as a compliment."

"Please do." She reached up and touched his cheek. "I wish . . . I wish that I was Irma."

"Why?"

Her eyes dropped and her cheeks flushed with color. "So that I could *know* you like she does."

Longarm sucked in a deep breath and surprised himself by blurting out, "Caroline, I'm not sure that that would be such a good idea."

"Why not?" she asked, suddenly looking up at him and placing her hands on his broad shoulders.

"Because I'm not the gentleman you think I am," he confessed. "I've a lot of the animal in me. If I didn't have that, I would have been killed years ago."

She swallowed hard, and he knew that her next words were difficult and came from the heart.

"And what if I told you that even aristocratic women have a little bit of the 'animal' buried deep inside of them? And that they aren't ashamed of it and even desire it at times."

Longarm reached out and pushed the door shut. He took Caroline in his arms and kissed her deeply, passionately, and she reacted like any healthy young woman who had ever been attracted to him. Caroline's lips were soft and her body was even softer. Longarm heard a moan escape her and he reached down to unbutton her dress, but Caroline suddenly broke away.

"No," she whispered.

"Why not?"

"Because of Irma. She's my friend."

Longarm expelled a deep breath. "Yes," he said, "and mine. I care for her."

"Then . . . then there is nothing more to say, is there?"

"I don't think so," he reluctantly agreed. "But you

must have known this would happen if you came to my compartment."

"I was hoping just to apologize."

He took her into his arms and kissed her mouth again, only this time gently and without a great hunger surging up in his loins. "I don't believe that for a single moment, Lady Caroline. I think you wanted to make love, but had a sudden and massive attack of guilt."

She smiled. "Are you always so brutally honest with ladies who find you irresistible?"

"No."

"I don't know whether to feel happy or sad that you were with me, but I'm glad to have kissed you, Marshal. After I've long been back in England and most of the memories of this great adventure have faded, I'll still remember and treasure these moments. And if I someday have children, when I am old and they are courting, I'll tell them about the handsome and brave United States marshal who risked his life for us and whom I kissed and desired with all my heart."

Longarm smoothed his mustache. "You had better get out of here while you still can."

"Let's not let Irma know we had this conversation and a kiss."

"Of course not."

"Would you ever . . ."

"What?"

"Consider marrying her?"

"No."

"Why not? Irma is pretty and good. She's smart and I think she is wonderful. Marshal, I was very much hoping that you shared that conclusion."

"I do," he said. "It's got nothing to do with Irma and

everything to do with me. I couldn't ask a woman to marry me given the kinds of things that I have to do in my line of work."

"Like shooting men before they shoot you."

"Exactly."

"Very sensible," she said, turning to leave.

"Caroline. May I ask you a personal question?"

She turned back. "Of course."

"Why are you out here?"

"My husband died last year."

"I'm sorry."

"Me too. I needed to get away, and that's why I've come out here to really experience the American West. To partake in your great adventure while there is still time."

"With that controlling old woman who orders you about as if you were working for her, instead of the other way around?"

Caroline's brow knitted. "Marshal, that 'old woman' is actually my aunt. Only she prefers to be thought of as an ordinary woman."

Longarm didn't understand this. "Why?"

"Because she feels that if people don't think of her as aristocracy, they will be more open and honest and she can judge them better."

"I see. And what does she think of me?"

"She thinks you are very dangerous for me."

"And you agree?"

Caroline laughed softly. "After that kiss, I *know* that you are very dangerous. Good-bye, Marshal."

"Good-bye," he said wistfully.

Chapter 7

The rest of the train ride into Reno was blessedly uneventful. Longarm thought about Lady Caroline more than he should have, and maybe Irma sensed that, because her passion cooled and she spent more time in her second-class coach. Twice when Longarm came by to visit, he found Irma engaged with a handsome young merchant named Sam Allen who owned a big granary and feed store in Reno.

"I sell a complete line of Stetsons too," Sam said, poking a finger at the hole in Longarm's hat. "I could take that one in on trade and give you a new one for . . . oh, twenty dollars."

"Thanks, but no thanks," Longarm said.

"Sam is very seriously thinking about opening a second store in Carson City," Irma said, looking quite excited as she sat close to the enterprising young businessman. "What do you think, Custis?"

"I think that would probably be a fine idea."

"The deal pencils out," Sam said, actually reaching for a pad of paper and pencil in his shirt pocket. "I've done the figuring about six or seven times over. My father founded the Reno store and then he passed it on to me. My mother lost her mind about two years later. I'm the only child. I wish I had a brother to help me run two stores."

"You'll find someone to help," Longarm said.

"I'm pretty good at figures," Irma blurted out.

Sam grinned. He was a big kid, deceptively simple-looking at first glance, until you talked to him for a few minutes and realized he was very sharp in business. "You are, Irma?"

"You betcha."

"Well, maybe when we get to Reno, you could come down to Carson and I'll show you the store I want to buy and renovate. I'll have to put about three hundred and sixty-five dollars into it, but I'm sure that I can recoup my investment the first quarter, and then begin to turn a profit. You see, I get all the best prices because I know which suppliers to deal with and which ones to avoid."

"I'd love to look at it, Sam." Irma glanced up at Longarm. "Isn't this exciting?"

"It is," Longarm said, trying to force a degree of enthusiasm into his voice. "Very exciting."

"Aw," Sam said with a shrug, "investing is just part of doing good business and it's all pretty cut and dried. You just figure your investment, the cost of your loans, how long you have to carry inventory and what that will cost, and then how much markup you can charge and still stay competitive. After that, you look at the figures and say yeah or nay."

"Humph," Longarm said, trying to sound impressed. "And here I thought business was complicated."

74

"Nope, not at all. Frankly, I've been at this for ten years, since I was thirteen. My father had me doing everything in his store, and by the time I was fifteen, I was in charge and making the decisions. So it's old hat to me."

"I can tell."

"And maybe, just maybe, I could do you a little better deal if you want to trade me that ruined hat. What size is it?"

"Seven and a quarter, but I'm not interested in trading it off."

"Not even if I gave you fifteen dollars? That'd be about *half* of what a new one costs."

"It'd still leave me eighteen dollars poorer," Longarm said. "Besides, I'm getting used to the extra ventilation."

Sam didn't see that Longarm was joshing him, but Irma did and she became a little irritated. "Sam is just trying to help you out, Custis. There's no reason to poke fun."

"I'm not poking fun," Longarm said, "but I'm not trading in this hat. It reminds me that I need to both duck and shoot a little quicker."

"Yeah," Sam said, looking very concerned. "Irma told me all about what happened in Elko. I was taking a nap and didn't even hear the gunshots, but I guess you really drilled them two Elko fellas dead center."

"They were tough customers," Longarm said, "who didn't know the meaning of the word surrender."

"Whew," Sam breathed, "just the thought of them laying their dirty hands on little Irma makes my blood begin to boil."

"Yeah, me too," Longarm said, feeling a sudden urge to leave the pair alone.

75

• • •

That afternoon Longarm met Caroline in the aisle, and was going to just say hello and pass on by, but the lady blocked his path. She actually looked upset. "Custis, are you avoiding me?"

"No."

"Lucille and I haven't seen Irma in two days."

"She's found another man," Longarm admitted. "I've been jilted for a feed store owner."

"Really?" Caroline brightened at this news.

"Really."

"Is he nice? Handsome? Tell me about him over supper tonight."

"All right," Longarm said, "but will Mrs. Addie appreciate my company?"

"She'll probably elect to have her meal brought to her compartment." Caroline looked deeply into his eyes. "Would that greatly disappoint you?"

"Can't say that it would."

"We can also talk about going out to see those wild horses you told me were to be found near Reno."

"Caroline, I've got a job to do first."

Her smile faded. "A dangerous one?"

"Yes," he admitted, "and very important."

"Will it take long?"

"A week or two. Maybe even longer."

Caroline took a deep breath, and it was then that he noticed her eyes were misty. "And I suppose that there is the . . . the possibility that you might . . . get . . . killed?"

Longarm heard the choke in her voice and was deeply moved. He took Lady Caroline in his arms and said, "I'll be all right. If you can wait, we'll go mustang hunting up around Pyramid Lake. It's a beautiful, ancient lake, and I know some Paiute Indians who will show us the country and take us right to where we can see plenty of wild horses."

"You do?"

"Yes."

She took a deep breath. "I'm going to wait for you, Custis."

"What about your aunt?"

"I've given that some thought too. I'm going to tell her to go on to San Francisco."

"She'd leave you?"

"I'll make sure that she does," Caroline said. "She treats me like a helpless child and I'm not really helpless at all. I want to become stronger. Like Irma. And to do that, I have to be allowed the freedom to take risks."

There was almost a pleading in Caroline's voice when she looked up at Longarm and said, "Doesn't that make sense?"

"Perfect sense," he assured her. "But what will you do in Reno for a couple of weeks or possibly even longer?"

"I've thought about that too. I may get a . . ." Caroline had to clear her voice. "I may actually get a job."

"A job?"

"Not a hard one," she quickly assured him. "A very proper job, of course."

"Of course," Longarm said with a grin.

"Would you take a little time and help me find one? Or perhaps you could just recommend me to someone."

"What can you do?"

That stumped Caroline, and Longarm could see sudden alarm fire into her eyes. "Never mind," he said quickly. "We can talk about all this over supper tonight. I'm sure that there is something that you can do to earn money."

"Good," she answered, looking relieved. "I'm afraid that I really have had a protected upbringing. It was not well received by my family when I announced that I was coming to America to see the Wild West."

"I'm sure it was not."

"They raised a terrible howl. They told me that I'd be scalped by Indians . . . and worse."

"What could be worse?"

"Well," she said, blushing, "you know."

"Oh, yes. I guess that would be worse than scalping."

"Custis, can you please tell me tonight exactly what you must do in Reno?"

"I'm afraid not. And besides, I'll be leaving that city almost immediately after we arrive tomorrow. Maybe after dinner, we could come back to my compartment and . . ."

She shook her head. "I don't think so. Not with the chance that Irma might come to say her good-byes."

"Very unlikely. She's really hooked a good fish this time. Sam Allen looks like he'd make a good husband."

"I hope so, for her sake. Irma told me that she didn't like men and trusted them even less, until she met you."

"Really?" Longarm was quite surprised to hear this bit of news.

"Oh, yes. She said that you had restored her faith in men."

"But she jilted me and found another."

"That's only," Caroline assured him, "because you are not ready for marriage."

"That's certainly true."

"Good-bye," Caroline said sweetly.

Longarm watched her walk up the aisle, liking the round of her bottom and the graceful way she moved. He was sorry that they would not have this night together, but he fully understood her thinking. It would be very awkward if Irma did show up at compartment number three and found them making love.

No, Longarm thought, it might be better to wait until they arrived in Reno and found separate but mutually accessible hotel rooms.

As their train pulled into Reno, Longarm remembered that the town had originally been a crossing for the overland wagon trains going over Donner or one of the other passes into California. When the Central Pacific Railroad had finally blasted over the Sierras with nitroglycerine and legions of hearty Chinese laborers, Reno had blossomed into a central distribution and shipping point for the western Nevada mines, and most especially for the fabulously wealthy Comstock Lode, which had been discovered in 1869. This was the same historic year that the transcontinental railroad had been completed and its rails joined at Promontory Point, Utah.

With the decline ten years later of the Comstock Lode, Reno's economy had shifted from its dependence upon mining and railroading to becoming a major shipping point not only for the nearby cattle ranches, but also for the huge timber companies that industriously logged the eastern slopes of the Sierra Nevada Mountains.

When the train jolted to a halt, Longarm helped Lady Caroline and her sour-faced aunt down from the train, and called for a carriage to take them to the Comstock

House, one of Reno's finest lodgings.

"When will I see you again?" Caroline asked anxiously as Longarm helped her into the carriage.

"I'll stop by later," he promised.

"All right."

The carriage moved away and when Longarm turned, he saw Irma and Sam also preparing to depart in a carriage. Irma, catching Longarm's eye, said something to her new beau and hurried over.

"I'm sorry about the way this worked out, Custis."

"I'm not," he said. "I like Sam and I hope you and him get hitched."

"We will," she vowed. "He's crazy about me. I'm going right to work for him, and I'll bet anything that we'll be man and wife within a month."

"I wouldn't take that bet," Longarm said with a laugh. "You are one determined woman when you get something in your mind. Besides, you'll make Sam a wonderful wife and mother to his children."

Irma hugged him so tightly that Longarm could feel her body trembling. "Custis, I can't believe how my life has changed so much for the better in just one week. That business in Cheyenne with Big J and the others, it all seems unreal and like a nightmare."

"It's done and you should forget it," Longarm told her. "You're starting all over fresh. New place, new time, new people."

"Thanks to you."

Longarm felt his own throat begin to ache, so he pushed her away and said, "Good luck."

"Will you come by Sam's store to visit after you're finished doing whatever it is you must do?"

"Of course."

"And swear to me that you won't get yourself killed?"

"I swear it," he said with a grin. "I won't let myself get killed."

"Good! Then I'll let you go."

Longarm stepped back, but no sooner had he done that than Irma reached out and anxiously grabbed his hand. "Custis, what happens if some of the men I knew in Cheyenne come here and see me? What if they tell Sam about my awful past?"

"Warn them that if they do, I'll return and shoot 'em dead," Longarm advised her with a straight face.

Her eyes widened. "You would?"

"Yes, just as dead as that pair in Elko."

Irma gulped, straightened, and said, "I believe you would do that for me, and if ever I should be threatened by my past, I will use your honorable name."

"Fair enough," Longarm said with a wink as he turned and headed into town.

Chapter 8

Marshal Gus Bell was a longtime acquaintance, and Longarm would not have even considered coming into Reno without paying him the courtesy of a professional visit. Bell was Longarm's age, and had a quiet, unassuming demeanor that Longarm appreciated. The man was extremely capable but never overbearing. In fact, although Bell was a large man, he had the knack of quietly slipping into the background until he was really needed.

Now, as they sat in Bell's office, the marshal of Reno was very attentive as Longarm explained why he had come to town dressed as a dandy hoping to pose as a businessman rather than being pegged as a United States marshal.

"Matthew Killion and his crowd have been rumored to be responsible for that train robbery," Bell observed, "but so far no one has been able to collect a shred of evidence against them."

"Why?"

"Killion is ruthless and tough," Bell replied. "He's also smart enough to be generous with the men who ride for him. They're loyal and close-mouthed. Killion makes sure that they don't get drunk outside of Helldorado and start wagging their tongues."

"I see." Longarm scowled. "What about his sons?"

"Clyde, the older one, is a would-be gunfighter. He's been in one damned scrape after the next, and he'll kill someone in cold blood one of these days and then even Killion and his lawyer friends won't be able to save him from a noose. I'd never turn my back on Clyde."

"And the younger one?"

Bell steepled his fingers and leaned back in his creaky old office chair. "Randy is different from either his father or his brother."

"How so?"

"Well, I got the feeling that, under that tough shell, he's a very decent kid. He's about seventeen, maybe eighteen, and I guess he was a damned bright student, from what I've been told by a schoolmarm who taught him to read and write up on the Comstock. I've been told the kid reads Shakespeare."

"Huh," Longarm mused. "That most certainly doesn't fit the family mold."

"No, and Randy has been known to be kind and generous. In fact, I've heard that he's actually kept his brother from shooting some people, a couple of helpless drunks and an old Chinaman who ruined Clyde's shirt after a washing."

"What's the kid doing in Helldorado?"

"What else does he know?" Bell asked, raising his hands. "Besides, you know how a kid that age would stick to his father and brother come hell or high water. I have a feeling that Randy could be saved if he was made to see the light in time. Otherwise, he'll get caught along with the others and stretch a rope before too many more years."

"It sounds like you know that kid."

"I've met him a time or two. He's quiet and no braggart like his father and his brother. He's the kind of a kid that you'd want for your own."

"Why do you suppose he has that goodness in him?"

"Randy's father had a Mexican woman for a couple of years. She was Matthew's mistress and everyone knew about her, but Killion pretended she didn't even exist. From what I hear, Randy came to look upon her like the mother he never knew."

"What happened to her?"

"I don't know," Bell said. "Her name was Lupe Sanchez and she was a real beauty. I guess she was about forty, but you'd never know from looking at her. She had a lot of class, and I never understood why she tolerated Killion. Anyway, she must have gotten fed up with him and his gang because she just disappeared."

"Do you think Killion killed her out of fear she'd talk to the authorities?"

"It's possible," Bell admitted. "After that train robbery, there were a lot of railroad and government officials nosing around looking to pin the job on the Killion bunch. I'm sure Lupe could have turned the gang in, but she never did."

"Maybe she was afraid he'd kill her and he did anyway."

Bell shrugged. "There are people who are searching for Lupe, but who knows? If I were to name the one person most likely to know her whereabouts, it would be Randy."

Longarm mused this over for a moment and said, "Any suggestions on how best I can get into Helldorado without being tagged as a lawman?"

"I don't know," Bell said. "Personally, I don't think you have a prayer of pulling this off. Your boss must have marbles in his head to send you into Helldorado, especially dressed up in that suit and looking like you have money."

This was not comforting news to Longarm. "I'm still asking for suggestions, Gus."

"Well, if you're bound and determined to get yourself killed in Helldorado, I'd suggest that you go in as a freighter or maybe a horse trader."

"A horse trader?"

"Sure. Don't you have some Paiute friends up by Pyramid Lake who you could talk into driving some mustangs into Helldorado, ostensibly to sell?"

"I sure do," Longarm said, "but I wouldn't want to risk their lives."

"I doubt that Matthew Killion would be stupid enough to take on the Paiutes. No, sir, he and his boys cross their land too often to risk that kind of thing. I'd say that you'd be safe enough if you could pose as a Paiute mustanger."

"That wouldn't work," Longarm snorted. "In the first place, the Paiutes are all well under six feet and I'm six-four. I'd stick out like a sore thumb."

"All right, then be a half-breed. Or better yet, a half-breed that is on the run from the law."

Longarm had been sitting astraddle a wooden chair with his arms draped over the back. Now, he stood up and began to pace. "Maybe it would work," he said. "I could trade in this suit for some hard-looking clothes and boots. George Two Ponies would lend me a horse and saddle, and we've ridden together enough so that I know what mustanging is all about."

"You'd need to trail at least a half-dozen trade ponies into Helldorado. Killion would laugh at 'em, but they'd get you into his town, and then you could stay for a couple of days and try to gain some evidence."

"By damn," Longarm said, "I think you've really hit on something. I'm surprised that I didn't think of anything this good myself."

"Well," Gus said modestly, "I've had quite a while to ponder on this and I told myself that, if I wasn't so damned well known in these parts, it's the disguise that *I'd* use. Which brings me to another point."

"And that is?"

"Are you sure that neither Matthew Killion nor any of his gang has seen you before?"

"I'm not sure of anything," Longarm admitted.

"Shave that mustache, get some old clothes, smear dirt on your face and look dark like a half-breed, and do a lot of praying."

"That's your advice?"

"It is."

"I'll take it, except for the mustache."

"Then use some charcoal or smoked Indian roots to make it black rather than brown," Bell advised. "And do the same for your hair. If you're supposed to be half Mexican or white and half Indian, you'd need to have black hair, black brows, and a black mustache."

"I guess that's true," Longarm reluctantly admitted.

"Damn right it is."

Longarm stood up and extended his hand. "I wish that you weren't tethered to Reno and could come with me."

"I don't," Bell said with a smile. "I enjoy living too much to do that."

"Thanks for the encouragement."

"Is there anyone that you want me to send your pension to after they string you up by the thumbs and slowly carve you into strips and leave you to hang in the sun until you're the color of old beef jerky?"

"No," Longarm said, not a bit amused, "but there are a couple of ladies who just arrived in your town that I wish you'd look out after."

"Are they young and pretty?"

"Would it matter?"

Bell shook his head. "Of course not. But it would help to make the job more pleasant."

"One is named Irma and she's on her way to snagging Sam Allen for a husband."

"Then I hope she's got a sense of humor."

"What," Longarm asked, "does that mean?"

"It means that Sam Allen doesn't have any sense of humor at all. He takes himself far too seriously."

"So I gathered," Longarm said. "And yes, Irma has a great sense of humor."

"Good-looking, huh?"

"Very. But she's got a past that could haunt her, Gus. And if it does, I want you to help her out."

"You mean . . ."

"I mean if you see she's not smiling, then find out why and solve the problem."

"I follow your drift," Gus said. "You know I don't hold a person's past against them. I'll help your lady friend. What about the other woman? I take it that she's also got some big problem that I need to help her with?"

"Her name is Lady Caroline."

87

Bell's eyebrows raised. " 'Lady' Caroline? You mean she's some kind of royalty?"

"Some kind of aristocracy. She's traveling with her aunt, who is also aristocracy but has the face of a sun-dried prune and the disposition of a skunk."

"So what are they doing here?"

Longarm told the marshal about how Caroline had defied her family to come in search of adventure and how her aunt had come along as the young woman's chaperone. He ended by saying, "Caroline thinks that she might like to work."

"You mean like *real* work?"

"Not hard work," Longarm corrected. "But she'd do well in a millinery, dress shop, or something of that nature. I expect she's very well educated and might also be able to work in a business office."

"I see," Bell replied. "So what are you asking me to do, help her find work?"

"Pay her a visit," Longarm suggested. "She's impressed by men with badges and authority. Probably has something to do with a strict aristocratic upbringing. Anyway, if she hasn't changed her mind and is still hoping for work, give her some introductions and encouragement."

"Sounds like the thing to do."

Longarm frowned. "By the way, Gus, you *are* still engaged to Miss Monroe, aren't you?"

"Nope," Gus said, not looking the least bit upset. "We broke it off. She wanted me to quit this office and go to work for her father in the feed store. I told her that I'd hate that line of work, and so she decided to look for a husband with a brighter future. But for a *lady* of the English court, I might just be willing to forsake this office and my huge salary of thirty-seven dollars a month."

"Now wait a minute," Longarm said. "If I'd have known you weren't engaged any longer, I doubt I'd even have said anything about Lady Caroline."

"I'm sure glad that you did, though," Gus said, grinning like an idiot. "I can hardly wait to see this woman. And Custis, you can rest assured that I'll do everything in my power to help her in each and every way that I can."

"Great," Longarm answered in a sour tone of voice.

"Anything else I can do for you today besides tell you what disguise to use and that I'll assist your lady friends?"

"No," Longarm said, "I think you've taken on quite enough already."

Gus laughed and came to his feet. He was a lean and handsome man and Longarm knew that, despite his talk, he was basically a shy person, but one that many women found very attractive.

"Good luck," Longarm said. "I'm going to find George Two Ponies and see if I can get him to help."

"He's a smart one," Gus said, "so I expect that he will, but it will cost the government a few dollars."

"It can afford it," Longarm told his friend as he headed out the door.

Longarm spent the next hour hunting up both Irma and Caroline to tell them that they had a friend in Marshal Bell. Both women seemed relieved, especially Irma, who said, "I just pray that I can get Sam hitched before anyone shows up that remembers me from Cheyenne."

"Your past is your past and your futures stretches out before you and the sun is shining."

89

"It is," Irma admitted. "But I sure will miss making love to you, Custis. I can't imagine that Sam could be anywhere near as good."

"Give him encouragement and teach him a few things, but not so fast that he gets suspicious."

"I will."

Lady Caroline hugged Longarm's neck and said, "I'll count the moments until you return."

"Have some fun and make some friends," Longarm advised. "The time will go faster and you'll enjoy yourself. Marshal Bell is a fine man."

"I'll look forward to meeting him," Caroline said, but her voice betrayed the sincerity of her words.

Longarm then visited the livery and rented a good horse and saddle.

"Any idea how long you'll be wanting them?" the liveryman asked just before he rode away.

"Depends on George Two Ponies," Longarm called back as he reined north toward the ancient Pyramid Lake.

Chapter 9

The Pyramid Lake Indians had always been a peaceful tribe, except for one notable occasion more than twenty years earlier, during the Pyramid Lake War of 1860. Longarm had actually talked to a few of the survivors of this war, and of course he was well acquainted with the Paiute version of it as told by men like George Two Ponies. The battle had started when a few disreputable whites kidnapped two young Indian girls and held them hostage at the William's Trading Station, about twenty-five miles west of the Comstock Lode on the Carson River.

The girls belonged to the Pyramid Indian tribe, and the Indians came to rescue them from the white men. In the process of freeing the girls, the Indians killed the three guilty whites and burned the station. Word of this slaughter quickly caused the whites to seek retaliation, especially in light of the rumor that a dozen white men had been killed and scalped and that five hundred Paiutes had gone on the warpath.

A force of young, untrained, and overzealous men marched north to seek revenge. They numbered just over a hundred, and because of their haste, ill-preparedness, and inexperience, were trapped by the waiting Indians and seventy-six men were killed. Only twenty-nine escaped the trap and lived to tell their story.

Panic ensued among the whites, and Longarm had heard that thousands of Comstock Lode miners fled over the Sierras to the safety of California, with entire mining settlements evacuated. A few months later, a huge battalion of trained soldiers along with five hundred volunteers returned to Pyramid Lake, where they soundly defeated the Indians, killing 160 of them. George Two Ponies himself was badly wounded in this terrible defeat and lost many of his family. After that, Fort Churchill was established to defend the territory against future Indian attacks. But the Paiutes, who had never sought trouble, buried their dead and remained in their sanctuary at Pyramid Lake, where they continued to raise corn as well as to fish and hunt in the marshes around the dead lake.

Whenever Longarm first saw Pyramid Lake, his mind was pulled back to a prehistoric time. The lake was huge, somewhat alkaline, and very still, except when the winds could whip the surface up to a froth. There were tall, majestic, and alkaline-crusted spires jutting out of the lake, and marshes where heron and migrating birds of all descriptions nested and fished.

Longarm was greeted warmly when he appeared at George's village, a small collection of huts on the southern end of the dead lake. George was short, like most Paiutes, and it was impossible to guess his true age. Longarm thought that the rotund and genial Indian was probably in his mid-forties, but George was extremely active and reputed to be one of the finest mustangers in the state of Nevada.

"Good to see you, old friend," Longarm said, dismounting from his rented horse to greet the Indian and his large family.

"Longarm," George said, his round face breaking into a wide, toothless smile. "Hi-ya!"

Longarm and George Two Ponies shared pleasantries for about an hour while the rest of the camp gathered around to listen and visit. Then, Longarm was escorted into George's wife's hut, which was made of sticks, reeds, and mud. They ate fish, wild goose, and some roots that Longarm found tasted very much like spinach. After the pipes were smoked and as the hour of darkness grew near, Longarm knew it was time to explain his mission.

"I have come to see my good friend George Two Ponies for friendship first, but also for the reason of money."

George, never one to avoid the white man's money, leaned forward over his fire and peered through smoke at Longarm. "Tell me of this money thing."

Longarm left out nothing. He was not surprised to learn that George had heard about the train robbery and the great amount of money that had been taken and still awaited recovery.

"We think it is a man named Killion. This man is very evil and he lives in a town called Helldorado, to the southeast two days ride from here."

"I know this place," George said, puffing his pipe and nodding solemnly. "It is bad."

"Yes," Longarm agreed, "I understand that Helldorado is a very bad place. This man, Matthew Killion, must be stopped. To do that, my friend, I have to get into Helldorado and they must think that I am evil, like them."

93

"What do you want of me?"

"Take me there. I am going to be a half-breed. A mustanger, like you. We will take mustangs and they will not see that I wear a badge."

George reflected on this for only about a second. "Killion kill George and take his ponies."

"No," Longarm said abruptly. "I promise that no harm will come to you."

"Ponies?"

"If they are stolen or run off or any harm comes to you, I will pay for them all."

George scowled as if he had bitten into a bitter root. Longarm knew that the Indian did not want to take his ponies into Helldorado, but that friendship also weighed very heavily.

"George," he said, "I need this favor. In return, I will pay you one hundred dollars."

Longarm wasn't sure where he would get the one hundred dollars. He had some money, but not enough, not even if he sold his Winchester repeating rifle and his Colt revolver, Ingersoll pocket watch with attached derringer, and every other damn thing he owned. But somehow, Longarm knew that he *would* find a way to scrounge up one hundred dollars, which was chicken feed considering that ten thousand dollars in stolen money were the stakes being played for in this deadly game.

George passed his pipe to Longarm saying, "You pay half money now. George no run out on friend."

"I know that," Longarm said, "but I don't have fifty dollars right now."

"Then how you get one hundred?"

"I can send for it over the talking wire."

"How do this?"

"It's . . . hard to understand," Longarm said, fumbling for words. "Actually, the money itself doesn't come over the wire, just the promise to pay."

"Who promise?"

"My boss, Marshal Billy Vail."

"Maybe he bring money to George Two Ponies and make happy."

"He's too far away."

"Then maybe should not give promise," George said after long reflection.

"Look," Longarm said, "I'll give you my rifle. A very good rifle."

When George remained wrapped in stony silence, Longarm reached into his pockets and pulled out a good folding knife and fifteen dollars. "My rifle, this knife, and money. What do you say, my friend. All this and more later only for helping me get into Helldorado without getting killed."

"Maybe," George said, coming to his feet. "Let you know tomorrow."

Longarm knew better than to argue or to rush George. If he had learned one thing about Indians, it was that they did not tolerate being crowded into important decisions. They made their decisions very slowly and carefully, and often only after consultation with the other members of their tribe, with special consideration for their wiser elders. Longarm was sure that his offer would precipitate a tribal council meeting and that the matter would be debated most of the long night.

"I need an answer by sunrise," Longarm told the Indian as he also came to his feet. "Yes or no. I need an answer by tomorrow at sunrise."

George didn't indicate that he had heard this deadline,

but Longarm was sure that he had. He followed George outside and they stood in the sunset of the day, watching liquid gold stain the calm surface of Pyramid Lake.

"How has the fishing been?" Longarm asked as evening laid a dark blanket across the eastern hills.

"Ask wife."

"Then how is the horse hunting?"

"Is good, when damn whites stay away from our land and the big mountains."

Longarm knew that "the big mountains" were the Ruby Mountains. He nodded with sympathetic understanding, and went to unsaddle his horse. But it was gone, and his saddle had been neatly placed under a pinyon pine. A young boy that Longarm judged to be about eleven years old stood guard, and Longarm went over to offer the kid a reward for his diligence and initiative.

"Thank you for unsaddling my horse and watching over my things," he said, knowing it was not necessary because no Indian would insult his fellow tribe members by doing the unthinkable of stealing from a friend and a guest.

The boy beamed.

"What's your name?"

The boy raised both hands upward, palms to the sky. He shrugged his shoulders, clearly not understanding the question.

"My name is Longarm," Longarm said, pointing at himself.

"Raul," the boy said, picking up Longarm's meaning.

"Are you a son of George Two Ponies?"

The boy was confused again because he did not know

the meaning of the word son and Longarm, dammit, could not think of a way to convey this meaning.

Longarm smiled at the kid and dragged some change out of his pockets. He extended it to the boy, who took the money, then smiled and handed it back.

"Then how about this," Longarm said, finding a piece of hard candy that he'd bought in Denver but had never gotten around to eating.

The boy took the candy and his eyes gleamed. He popped it into his mouth and grinned, then turned and went back into the camp and disappeared into George Two Ponies' hut.

"Yep, he was the son," Longarm said, untying his bedroll and spreading it on the ground.

Longarm was dog tired and he really was looking forward to sleeping under the stars, although the night would turn quite cold. No matter, he thought. His suit, his bedroll, and his horse blanket would be plenty enough to keep him warm.

In the morning, Longarm awoke to the feel of George's moccasined foot prodding him in the side. Longarm started, then sat up and knuckled his eyes. It was very cold, and a stiff wind did not make things any more comfortable.

"What?" Longarm asked.

"You give rifle and we go now."

"Good," Longarm said, "but can't we go into your hut first so that I can thaw out?"

George shook his head. "Go now."

"All right, but first I need to find some different clothes. And I need to color my hair black, like yours. Did I tell you all this yesterday?"

"No."

"Well, I'm supposed to look rough, like a mustanger." Realizing that he was very nearly insulting his host, Longarm quickly took a different angle. "I need to trade clothes and boots."

"Hat too?" George said hopefully.

"No!" Longarm lowered his voice. "Not the hat. Everything but this hat."

George took that bit of bad news without comment. He wheeled around and stomped back to his hut and Longarm, stiff, cold, and blowing into his frozen hands, followed.

Two hours later, Longarm had his black hair and old clothes. Had the weather been warm, he would have insisted that the clothes be boiled before he wore them because they would most certainly have been infested with body lice. But the weather was cold and the clothes were without lice. Just before leaving, Longarm tromped over to the lake and stared at his reflection in its cold, gray surface.

"Yep," he said, to himself, "I look rough enough to be an outlaw on the run or a mustanger. I look like anything but a lawman."

Longarm left his Ingersoll watch and derringer in George's hut. He hated to do that, but the type of man he was supposed to be would never carry a nice railroad pocket watch and gold watch fob.

"Let's go," he said to George. "Just show me my horse."

"That one," George told him, pointing to an ugly black gelding.

"He looks like a hard traveler."

"Is."

"Then how about something a little better?"

"No," George said with finality. "If bad man kills you, then takes your horse, maybe bad horse kill him some day."

"How comforting," Longarm said, reaching for his saddle.

Fifteen minutes later, they were riding out of the Paiute camp, heading southeast to intersect the Truckee River and angle farther south until they came to Helldorado. They were pushing mustang ponies, but they were all poor-looking beasts, with the exception of one handsome buckskin that was too skinny. These were the sorriest nags that George could collect in such a short period of time. Longarm knew that he wanted the very worst animals just in case they were both killed and the horses were kept by Killion or one of his men.

An unfortunate but distinct possibility.

Chapter 10

"There," George said, pointing toward the dozen or so buildings that were cradled in the lap of a collection of sagebrush-covered hills. "Helldorado."

"It isn't much, is it?" Longarm was not very impressed. The town had been half destroyed by a fire, and many of its buildings were now little more than charred ruins.

"Damn bad place," George Two Ponies grunted.

"Well," Longarm said, "if that's where I'll find Matthew Killion and the ten thousand dollars he stole from the train, then that's where I need to be. George, have you changed your mind about riding in there with me?"

"I go," George said, a moment before reining after a jug-headed mustang that seemed determined to escape and run back toward its home ground.

Longarm watched the Indian cut off the mustang's escape and then drive it back into the herd of horses that they had trailed down from Pyramid Lake. This was a poor bunch of mustangs and they looked awful, although Longarm was sure that wouldn't matter. The idea was to fool Killion into thinking that Longarm was a loser and a drifter, a man who was just hoping to make a few easy dollars off some rough Indian ponies. A man with a troubled past and with few prospects for the future, except perhaps if it was as a part of the Killion gang.

Longarm rode back over to the Paiute and said, "I have to be real honest with you, George. There could be men in this gang that recognize me even with my black hair and these old, ragged clothes. If there is, we're going to have to go to war."

"Maybe get killed quick, eh?"

"You're packing a six-gun, and I know you've got one hidden in your coat. Are you any good with them?"

"Pretty damn bad shot."

"I was afraid of that," Longarm said. "Well, if someone calls out my name and I go for my gun, I won't hold it against you if you were to spin that horse of yours around and ride like a bat out of hell."

"I run, all right," George said. "No use dying for white man's trouble."

"You're right," Longarm said. "And so I won't expect you to do anything else. You've got a wife and kids."

The Indian nodded in stern agreement and rode off to drive his horses into the small, brush-choked valley that held the town of Helldorado.

Longarm was tense as they approached the outlaw stronghold of Helldorado, but he felt confident that he would not be recognized. With his hair dyed black from the burned roots of a creosote bush, and wearing the old floppy hat he'd borrowed from a Pyramid Lake Paiute, Longarm was sure that he would not be pegged as a lawman. He looked exactly like an outlaw on the run who was dabbling with mustangs while trying to figure out a way to stage a robbery.

As they neared the town, Longarm could see that

Helldorado had once been a pretty substantial town. There were three big, two-storied buildings made of stone, and the ruins of what had probably been a business district that had been ravaged by a fire, not an uncommon experience in these mining towns where water was scarce, liquor fueled fools, and there was usually not even a volunteer fire department until after the town had been razed.

Someone, perhaps Matthew Killion, had rebuilt some of the buildings and shops. There were several large corrals and even a wagon yard, although must of the wagons were dismantled and totally inoperative.

"Looks rough," Longarm said. "I wonder how many outlaws Killion has living here."

George shrugged, either to say he did not know or simply did not care.

"Okay," Longarm said to his stoic companion, "here comes the chamber of commerce to welcome us."

About ten hardcases materialized from the saloon to form a line and block their progress. All ten of the men were heavily armed.

"You recognize any of them as Matthew Killion?" Longarm asked out of the side of his mouth.

"No. Big one with red shirt and black pants is son."

"That would be the mean one, Clyde," Longarm said to himself as he judged the young man. Clyde was as tall as Longarm, but not as broad-shouldered. He was wearing a tie-down holster low on his thigh, and a sneer pulled his mustache down at the corners of his mouth. Clyde's face was square and brutish, and the men flanking him were of the same disreputable-looking type. Any one of them looked as if they'd cut their own mother's throat for a peso.

"Far enough!" Clyde commanded. "Just turn them jug-headed sonsabitches around and get them out of here before I make 'em all buzzard bait!"

"Hold up there!" Longarm shouted, prodding his horse forward and reining around the mustangs. "We came to sell you boys some horses. They's real cheap!"

Clyde threw his head back and guffawed, sounding like the braying of a sick mule. Longarm forced a smile and tried to look dumb and happy. "Howdy, boys! I got some good mustangs for sale and you won't find 'em any cheaper."

Clyde stopped laughing and stepped out in front of the others. "I said for you and that Injun to turn them nags around and ride out before I shoot 'em!"

Longarm reined up short. He knew that he had to somehow gain an invitation to Helldorado, and Clyde sure wasn't making the task any easier. Not knowing what else to do, Longarm dismounted. He would continue to play it dumb and innocent.

"Me and George are hungry and thirsty. So's these fine horses we're selling so cheap."

"Food and water don't come free," Clyde said. "We got hay and grain, food for you and the Injun too, but everything costs plenty out here in Helldorado."

"We got money," Longarm said, "and I'm willin' to pay a fair price. How about we corral and take care of these ponies and then we help ourselves to some whiskey?"

"How much money do you have?" Clyde asked. "Probably not more than fifty cents between you, judging from your outfits."

"Oh, no!" Longarm protested. "We sold some ponies in Carson City and I got almost a hundred dollars."

Clyde's eyebrows shot up. "A hundred dollars?"

"Yes, sir!"

"Let's see the color of it."

Longarm dug into his pants and came up with a wad of greenbacks. He made sure that he kept them in his left hand while his right hand stayed very close to the butt of his six-gun as he said, "Mister, I told you we have cash money."

"And so you do," Clyde said. "I guess that it wouldn't hurt anything for you to ride in, provided you enjoy a friendly game of poker."

Longarm didn't want to appear too eager or too stupid. "Well, sir, we'll play a little poker but I won't gamble everything. We've been mustanging for near on three months and it's getting to be winter. Got to find a warm place to winter in this year and need some money for eats and such."

"Bring your money and your ponies," Clyde ordered. "We'll sit you beside a potbelly stove and we'll pour you good whiskey and you can show us the color of your money. But the Injun, he stays outside."

Protest flared in Longarm's eyes. "But he likes whiskey as much as me."

"He can drink in the street or in the livery barn," Clyde said in a hard voice, his eyes challenging either Longarm or George Two Ponies to make an issue of this decree.

"Yes, sir," Longarm said. "But I sure hope we can sell you some ponies. They may not look like much, but they're sound and George can break 'em to ride."

"I wouldn't be seen on one of them sorry bastards," an outlaw growled.

Longarm managed to look chagrined, and then he

climbed back on his own horse. The ten men parted and allowed the mustangers and their weary ponies to pass on to a big corral.

"Will this be all right?" Longarm asked, struggling hard to sound meek.

"Sure."

"Gonna need some water buckets and hay."

"You'll get 'em," Clyde said. "Pen them mustangs and we'll worry about taking care of them later."

Longarm nodded in ready agreement, knowing that his Paiute friend George would not abandon the mustangs until they were well fed and watered.

When Longarm stepped down from his horse, a young man in his teens appeared to open the gate to the pen. He nodded in silent greeting to Longarm, and held the gate open until all the mustangs were inside.

"I guess I might as well unsaddle our horses and turn them in with the others," Longarm said as he dismounted.

"If I were you, mister," the kid said softly, "I'd keep my saddle on and my cinch tight."

Longarm knew at once that this was the youngest Killion, the kid named Randy who the marshal in Reno had said was a breed apart from his father and older brother.

"Why's that?" Longarm asked.

"In case you or the Indian decide to leave real sudden," Randy said quietly.

"And why would I want to do that?"

"You just might."

"Hell, kid, I'm hear to stay for a while. Me and George are plumb worn down to nothing." Longarm turned and surveyed the fire-ravaged and blackened town. "You must have had a hell of a fire here not so long ago."

"Been a couple of years," Randy said. "That was before my father took over Helldorado for good."

"Helldorado," Longarm repeated. "I like the sound of that. How'd it get its name?"

"There was once a lot of gold found right here, but even then, it was miserable as hell," Randy said. "Now, if you've asked enough questions, I reckon you best get some eats and then play poker."

Longarm ducked his head behind his horse and untied the cinch. He dragged the saddle off and tossed it up on the cedar-pole fence. He led his horse into the pen and turned it free with the mustangs as George brought over the first of many buckets of water that he would tote for the thirsty horses.

"Say," Longarm said out loud enough for everyone to hear, "how come everyone here is so eager for me to play poker? You boys wouldn't be thinking I'm going to play against a stacked deck, are you?"

Longarm asked the question with an easy, temper-diffusing grin that kept anyone from taking serious offense.

"Hell, no!" Clyde said. "If we wanted your money that bad, we'd just shoot you. Don't need to go to all the bother of cheating to get your money."

"Glad to hear that," Longarm said, looking nervous.

"Come along," Clyde ordered. "I want you to meet the man in charge."

"Thought *you* might be in charge," Longarm said.

"I will be some day," Clyde said, puffing up like a pigeon. "But right now, this town belongs to my pa. He sets the rules and he decides who can come and who can go . . . on their feet or on a slab."

"I see," Longarm said. "And what is this gentleman's name?"

"Matthew Killion. *Mister* Matthew Killion."

"Yes, sir."

They didn't go far. Longarm was ushered into a hotel. He was escorted across a lobby that was nicely decorated, and saw several painted ladies keeping company with members of the gang.

"My father's office is upstairs," Clyde said, motioning Longarm to climb the stairs.

Longarm was in too deep to worry about getting shot in the back. He mounted the stairs and waited as Clyde moved ahead to knock on a door.

"Mister Killion?"

What kind of a son called his own father "mister," Longarm wondered.

"What is it!"

"We got a stranger that wants to sell us some mustangs."

"We don't need any!"

"He's got some money to spend."

A long pause. Then: "Send him in."

"He'll see you now," Clyde said, batting off Longarm's hat and pushing open the door.

Longarm wasn't prepared for either the man, his mistress, or the plush surroundings that Killion enjoyed. The room was big, maybe three hundred square feet, and it was decorated with beautiful dark wood that was polished to a shine. The furniture was heavy, and it looked to be imported from Europe. There was a long bar at one end of the room, stocked with expensive liquor. Across the other wall was an enormous couch, red and velvet, which a stunning young woman decorated with her scantily clad body. She wore a half smile and had bold, black eyes. Longarm thought her French, or maybe black Irish.

Matthew Killion was seated behind a huge oak desk. He was a very big man who had a wide rack of shoulders and hair that was starting to turn salt-and-pepper. He had the same lantern jaw that he'd passed on to both sons, and his eyes were penetrating as they sized up Longarm.

"Who are you?"

"Name is Custis," Longarm said, wringing his hat in his hand. "I been mustanging with a Paiute Indian and heard that your men needed horses."

"His horses are worthless," Clyde told his father. "Only an Indian would be seen on one of 'em."

Matthew nodded ever so slightly. He returned his eyes to Longarm and said, "My son says that we can't do business, Custis. However, I understand that you do have funds."

"Funds?"

Killion's voice took on an impatient edge. "Money."

"Yes, sir, Mr. Killion, but like I told your son, we came to *make* money selling you horses, not to lose what little we have at your poker table."

"Sometimes a man finds that he has to change his plans. Take out your money and put it on my desk."

Longarm's jaw dropped. "Sir?"

"I said, put your money on my desk."

When Longarm hesitated for just a fraction of a second, Clyde's gun jumped into his hand and its barrel jabbed hard into Longarm's spine. "You heard Mr. Killion! Empty your damned pockets!"

Longarm did. He had not actually been aware of how

much money he had, but Clyde counted out seventy-three dollars and then said to his father, "He's also got horses and saddles. What do you want us to do with him and the Paiute? Kill 'em?"

"Oh, now wait a minute!" Longarm choked. "We came here to do an honest business. We didn't do anything wrong. Now why would you want to go and kill us?"

For a heart-stopping moment Killion seemed to consider the question, and then he smiled. "We don't want to kill you, Custis. But everything is expensive out here, so we'll hold onto your money against the expenses and any gambling debts that you might run up in Helldorado. Before you leave tomorrow, we'll fairly settle the account. You have my assurance about that."

Longarm swallowed. "I guess that would be fair," he managed to say. "Yes, sir. That would be fair."

"Good," Killion said, turning his eyes toward the stunning blonde who was draped across his couch and pretending to be too bored to listen to their conversation. "Now, you can go down and enjoy yourself, Custis, while I enjoy myself."

"Yes, sir!" Longarm dared to shoot a quick glance at the young woman. She was enough to make a man's heart skip a beat. Her legs were long and shapely and shaded by black silk stockings. Her bosom was about to burst from her bodice, and her lips were cherry red. She was far, far more desirable than most of the girls on the frontier. Prettier than Irma, and arguably the equal of Lady Caroline. But just looking at her, Longarm could tell that she was as cold and dispassionate as a cat. He had the feeling that, if Clyde had shot him in the gut and he'd fallen to writhe out his final moments in screaming agony, this girl would have yawned.

"I said you could go," Killion said with a hard edge in his voice.

"Yes, sir!" Longarm pivoted on his heels and marched back outside. Clyde followed, and closed the door behind him.

"Custis?"

Longarm turned to confront the older Killion son. "Yeah?"

Clyde's hand streaked out and the back of it slammed into the side of Longarm's face so hard he staggered. He started to ball his fists, but checked that impulse just in time. "What the hell did you do that for?"

"For staring at Desiree. You're lucky my father didn't have you castrated."

Longarm wiped blood from his lips with the back of his sleeve. "Hell, man, I just looked at her!"

"If you ever look at her that way again, I'll kill you with or without my father's orders. Understood?"

It was all that Longarm could do to nod his head and then stomp back down the stairs.

Chapter 11

Even a good player, such as Longarm considered himself to be, didn't have much of a chance in a game of marked cards. He'd seen the marks, and they weren't even all that professionally done. Just some filling in of the squiggles on the backs of the cards so that the Killions knew who held face cards and could bet accordingly. Longarm would have loved to just grab those marked cards and cram them down Clyde's throat, but that would result in a bloody gunfight and he was determined to avoid that at all costs.

It galled Longarm terribly to be slapped and then cheated by a crowing, braying fool, but Longarm knew that he was playing for far bigger stakes than the measly dollars he was being cheated out of this night.

"Well, boys," he said later that night. "I've just got about ten dollars left and I'm going to have to quit."

"Who said?" a man named Dean wanted to know. "In Helldorado, you quit a card game when you're told to and not before."

Longarm glanced at Clyde, who took a sudden interest in his winnings. That told Longarm that Dean was acting on his own and that Longarm was probably being tested. If he backed down from Dean, he might as well tuck his tail between his legs and let them run him out of Helldorado tonight.

A fierce sense of joy filled Longarm as he realized that here, at last, was a challenge that he did not have ignore. And so he stared at Dean with more anticipation than anger. The man was big, coarse, and itching for a fight that Longarm was more than happy to provide.

Longarm pushed to his feet. "I'm quitting *now*," he said evenly.

All conversation in the saloon stopped. The men at the poker table who had smugly collected Longarm's dollars with their poorly marked cards grinned, probably expecting Dean to dismantle the scruffy-looking mustanger who had ridden into their town. A good, brutal whipping was their idea of great fun.

"What did you say?" Dean asked, coming to his own feet with his hands balled into big fists.

"I said don't push me, Horse Face."

Dean's jaw dropped. Up to this point, Longarm had been the model of servitude. This talk just didn't fit the image he'd carefully crafted in order to lower their guard.

Dean brushed back the hem of his coat to expose a well-worn Colt. "You're gonna get down on your knees and beg for your worthless life or I'm going to shoot you full of holes."

Longarm pushed back his own coat. He had a feeling that Dean was as fast with his gun as he was good with his fists. Either way, he was not a man to be taken lightly, and Longarm was going to have to either kill or completely humble the arrogant outlaw.

"If you want to spend the rest of your life in a pine box, make your play," Longarm said easily.

A flicker of doubt crossed Dean's eyes. He wasn't a coward and was confident of his ability, but Longarm knew the man would have preferred to have bluffed his way to victory rather than risk a bullet.

Clyde collected his own winnings and pushed back his chair. "I think I'll get out of the way," he said to no one in particular.

The others had the same idea, and their table emptied. Other tables emptied too as men quickly left the line of fire. Longarm could feel his blood starting to pound because nothing was certain in a gunfight other than that someone was probably going to die.

"Well?" Longarm asked.

When Dean gulped and then nervously glanced around as if seeking support, Longarm casually reached down with his left hand and brought his whiskey to his lips. He never took his eyes off those of the man he faced, and he barely sipped his drink before lowering it with a thin, half-smile.

"Well, Dean," he asked again in an entirely pleasant tone of voice. "What the hell is holding you up? Got a streak of yellow running up and down your spine?"

Beads of sweat burst out across Dean's forehead and his fingers waved over his gun butt. "I'm going to gut-shoot you, mister. I'm going to see you die slow!"

Longarm lowered his glass a little. "Go on," he urged. "Make your play."

Dean went for his gun. Longarm saw his eyes blink even as the man's hand dropped to his Colt. Longarm flicked the whiskey into Dean's eyes, then grabbed the edge of their poker table and pushed it hard into the outlaw. The edge of the table caught the hammer of Dean's gun as he blindly struggled to bring it up to fire. The gun fired harmlessly into the sawdust-covered floor, and then Longarm was heaving the table through and over the falling outlaw.

The whiskey had blinded Dean, and he was trying to wipe his vision clear when Longarm lashed out with a boot that caught him under the chin and snapped his head back. Dean rolled and Longarm kicked his forearm, sending the man's gun flying.

"Get up," he calmly ordered, waiting for Dean to struggle to his feet.

Dean was smart enough to take his time. He blinked, and then dried his eyes with his sleeve. When his vision was clear enough to see that Longarm hadn't even drawn his gun, Dean cursed and charged, arms reaching out to encircle Longarm and tackle him to the ground.

Instead, Longarm jumped aside and booted Dean in the ear. The man screamed in pain and furrowed through the dirty sawdust. Longarm walked over and grabbed his collar, dragging him to his feet.

"You were going to gut-shoot me, huh?" he asked, driving a powerful uppercut to Dean's belly that lifted him completely off the ground.

Still clutching the man's collar, Longarm pounded him again in the belly, and then grabbed Dean's ears and jerked the man's face down to connect with a wicked left uppercut. Everyone in the room heard Dean's nose pop, and then heard the man scream in agony as he crashed over a chair.

Longarm was feeling good, and he wasn't nearly ready to see this fight end. Not after all the sucking up he'd been forced to do to this gang. "Come on, Dean!" he urged.

"Get up and let's make a good fight of it!"

But Dean was finished. His face was a sheet of blood and he couldn't seem to get enough breath in his lungs. Longarm went over to help him into a chair, but Randy Killion stepped between them. Longarm hadn't a clue as to where he'd come from or how long he'd been in the saloon, but he was suddenly there and a gun was in his fist pointing at Longarm's chest.

"Dean has had enough fighting," Randy said, cocking his gun.

Longarm was brought up short. He forced a smile. "I was going to help him into a chair and maybe buy him a drink to show there were no hard feelings on my part."

"He doesn't need a drink," Randy said. "And there *will* be hard feelings."

Longarm raised his hands and unclenched his big fists. "It was a fair fight. He asked for it, not me."

"The man didn't have a chance," Randy said, "and we both know it."

"Where did you learn to fight like that?" Clyde asked, coming to stand beside his younger brother.

Longarm looked around at the others, then turned back to face the Killion brothers. "I had a friend that shared a cell block with me at the Yuma Territorial Prison. He was a former bare-knuckles champion and he knew how to use his fists. He beat the hell out of me the first two years we were locked up together."

"And then?" Randy asked.

"And then I learned the hard way and beat the hell out of him for a couple of years before we became friends."

The brothers exchanged quick glances. Clyde studied

115

Dean, and when he looked up at Longarm, there was respect in his deep-set eyes.

"Maybe I'd like a few lessons myself someday, Custis," Randy said. "And maybe I can teach you a few things that fella didn't know about fighting."

"I'm always happy to learn," Longarm said. "Shall we go to it right now?"

"No," Randy said quickly. Too quickly. "Maybe . . . maybe tomorrow."

"I'm going to be leaving Helldorado tomorrow," Longarm said, "unless you have changed your mind and decided to buy some of our ponies after all."

"Not very damned likely," Clyde said.

"There is one horse I kind of admire," Randy said.

Longarm turned his attention to the kid. "You'd be referring to the buckskin."

"That's right. He doesn't even belong with those others. Is he really a mustang?"

"No," Longarm said. "I figure he was a saddle horse that broke free and then went wild. He was running with the mustangs and we just brought him along."

"He's handsome," Randy said. "How much?"

"For you, ten dollars."

It was a ridiculously low price, one that Longarm knew the kid from Helldorado could not afford to pass up.

"Is he still rideable?"

"I don't know," Longarm said honestly. "But the Indian will know."

"Then let's talk to him now," Randy said.

Longarm looked at the others, and when Clyde did not object, he gave them a simple smile and followed Randy out the door, sucking on the knuckles that he'd barked.

"Are you as good with a six-gun as you are those fists?" Randy asked.

"Nope."

Randy stopped and looked at him. "I'm not sure that I or anyone else that saw you whip Dean believes that."

"Like I said," Longarm answered, "I had this friend in the Yuma prison."

"When were you there?"

"Got out last summer."

"And you were there at least four years?"

"Closer to five," Longarm lied.

"For what?"

"Killing a man over a deck of cards as poorly marked as the ones that we were just playing with."

Randy blinked. "If you knew they were marked, why did you play?"

"I didn't have much choice, now, did I?"

"No," Randy said, "I guess not. Is Custis your real name?"

"Yep."

"I doubt it," Randy said, then quickly added, "But I'm not calling you a liar."

"Sounded like it."

"Let it go," Randy warned. "If you kill or whip me, my pa and my brother will make you wish you'd never been born."

"Is that how it goes with you, kid? You just rely on your pa and big brother to back up your play?"

Randy was stung by the insult and he whirled on Longarm. "Are you forgetting that I just had a gun in my hand aimed at your heart and that I could have shot you?"

"Yeah," Longarm admitted, "I did forget. Thanks for

117

not drilling me. But why didn't you?"

"I don't kill men unless I have to." Randy relaxed. "And besides, I like that buckskin."

"Then let's go talk to George about him," Longarm suggested.

Ten minutes later, they were rousing George out of a deep sleep. The Indian fumbled for his gun, but Longarm pinned his wrists to the ground, saying, "It's all right, George. It's me, Custis."

The Paiute shook free and sat up. He started to speak, then saw Randy and changed his mind.

"This is Randy and he's all right," Longarm said in the way of an introduction. "He likes that buckskin and wants to know if the horse is broke to ride."

"No."

"Damn," Randy swore. "I'm not sure that I want to break him. Leastways, not in front of the others. If I get bucked off and land on my head, I'll never hear the end of it."

"You don't have to buy the horse," Longarm said, wanting to give the kid an honorable out. "Why don't you just think about it tonight and then we can talk in the morning before George and me leave?"

"Sounds good," Randy said. He walked over to the corral and draped his arms across the top rail. He watched the buckskin for several minutes and then he said, "That horse is about two hundred pounds light. How old do you think he is, George?"

"Six, maybe seven."

"He looks younger," Randy said. "You can tell by his teeth and we'll have a look at 'em in the morning. I may still buy him from you."

118

"That'd be dandy," Longarm said, "seeing as how I'm almost dead broke now."

"This hasn't worked out so good for you, has it?"

"Nope."

Randy frowned. "Let me tell you something, Custis, or whatever your name is. You're just damned lucky—far luckier than you can imagine—that you're still alive. And my advice is to get out of Helldorado as fast as you possibly can."

"Thanks."

"Here," Randy said, dragging out a few rumpled dollars. "I'm going to buy your horse for ten dollars because he doesn't belong in the company of those sorry mustangs. And if you're gone before daylight, just leave the buckskin in the corral and I'll take my chances with him tomorrow."

"Sounds more than fair," Longarm said, taking the money. "Thanks."

"Just leave Helldorado while you can," Randy said again, this time to them both before he walked away.

Longarm watched the kid go back into the saloon. Turning to George, he said, "That kid sure doesn't belong with this crowd of thieves and cutthroats."

"Don't trust kid," George warned. "Blood thicker than liquor."

"Yeah," Longarm said, not sure that he got the Paiute's meaning. "But that kid deserves a chance to get out of this mess before he is brought to a sad end."

George didn't say anything, and Longarm walked over to the corral and stared at the buckskin. It was the one good horse in the band, although it was thin and you had to look beyond its current condition to see its true quality.

"The kid has a good eye for horseflesh, George."

"Maybe."

"And maybe you should ride out tonight."

"What about wild horses?"

"Take 'em back to Pyramid Lake," Longarm said. "They've served their purpose."

George thought hard about that for a few minutes, and then he shook his head. "I go when you go," he said before he lay back down in his blankets and immediately began to snore.

Chapter 12

Longarm did not sleep particularly well that night. He couldn't help but wonder if Dean would recover enough to come looking to even the score. Longarm had rarely delivered such a savage beating, but he'd been in a fighting mood and he'd wanted to leave no doubt in anyone's mind that he was not quite the bumpkin that his clothes and easygoing manner had initially suggested.

Randy, of course, would tell his father and others about Longarm's supposed imprisonment in Yuma, and Longarm thought that someone in the gang might eventually check that out and discover it to be pure fabrication. But by then, Longarm was confident that he would already have broken the Killion gang and put them permanently behind bars.

"Still hanging around, huh?" Randy said, coming over to join them bright and early the next morning. "I thought you had enough sense to get out of Helldorado while the getting was good."

"Maybe your father will change his mind and decide to buy our mustangs after all."

"Not a chance."

"*You* did."

"Even you admitted that my buckskin isn't a mustang." Randy was dragging a saddle. "You fellas going to sleep all day, or are you going to help me saddle and shake out the buckskin?"

"If there's a breakfast in it for the trouble, we'll help you," Longarm said, looking at George Two Ponies, who nodded in agreement. George and Longarm had not eaten well since leaving Pyramid Lake.

"Fair enough," Randy said. "I was hoping one of you was handy enough with a rope to catch him and then help hold him steady while I cinch him up good and tight."

"I forgot to bring a rope," Longarm said, "and so did George."

"I'll get one for you," Randy said, dropping his saddle and wheeling around to march toward the town's livery.

"Why hurry?" George asked. "Eat first, then ride buckskin."

"That would be my choice too," Longarm said. "Only we aren't calling the turns. Let's just do things his way."

George nodded with reluctant agreement. He looked at Longarm with pity and then asked, "Can't rope horse?"

"No," Longarm said a little defensively. "I've never claimed to be a cowboy or a mustanger. How good are you with a rope?"

"Pretty damned good."

"I'm glad to hear that," Longarm said. "It wouldn't ring very true if we're supposed to be mustangers and neither one of us could even lasso a half-tame horse in a small corral."

"Yeah, I suppose not."

Randy came back while Longarm was tying up his bedroll and pulling on his boots. He looked at the kid and said, "How come you're so eager to get that buckskin rode?"

"I just like to take care of my business."

Randy handed the lariat to George, who shook it out and took a few practice whirls. "Too damned stiff," the Indian complained.

"It's a good grass rope," Randy argued.

George finished pulling on his own boots. He jerked his sagging pants up and tightened his belt, then shook out a loop and squeezed through the corral poles. Almost at once the mustangs begin to mill nervously about. Longarm had seen enough cowboys rope horses to know that they usually threw an overhand loop that sort of flipped up and then dropped down on the head of horse, often the one hiding somewhere in the rear of the band.

But George held his loop lower, and as he made his way into the center of the pen, the mustangs began to race around and around him in a panic-driven circle. Suddenly, a clear shot to the buckskin materialized and George's arm darted forward as quick as the head of a snake. Longarm saw that he was throwing an underhanded catch loop called the *mangana* that had been adopted from the Mexican *vaqueros* and was so difficult to throw correctly that it marked an expert roper.

The *mangana* loop snaked out about knee high and then, even as Longarm watched with admiration, the loop captured the buckskin's forefeet and tightened like the jaws of a bear trap. George threw his hip into the rope and planted his moccasins.

The buckskin's forefeet were jerked completely under its body and the animal did a somersault and landed on its back, its head slamming to the earth. While it was dazed and had the wind knocked from its body, George ran forward and quickly tied the animal's forelegs to its hind legs yelling, "Saddle!"

Randy brought the saddle over, and they loosened the ropes enough so that the buckskin could climb shakily to its feet. The dazed animal tried to run, but George used his rope to drop the buckskin hard to its knees.

"Got it!" Randy said, tightening the cinch and leaping into the saddle as George allowed the buckskin to climb back to its feet.

"Quirt him!" George yelled.

But Randy said, "If he isn't of a mind to buck and raise hell, I'm not going to—"

The buckskin snapped out of its daze and exploded into the sky. It took three huge hops and every time it landed, the horse did so on stiff legs. Randy's head snapped back and forth violently, and he began to spur and quirt at each buck. George ducked back out of the corral and coiled his rope while Longarm just stood back and admired the contest.

Randy was tossed high into the air. He landed flat on his back, the breath whooshing out of his lungs. Longarm jumped back into the corral and dragged the kid to his feet. "It's all right. That buckskin is a real tough horse."

"Catch him up," Randy choked. "We're just getting acquainted."

Longarm didn't have too much trouble grabbing the trailing rope and hauling the buckskin to a standstill. The animal was winded, but there was still fire in his eyes.

"Randy, are you sure you don't want to wait for the fog to clear from your brain?"

"Nope," Randy said, not aware that a crowd was gathering to watch the show. "Hold his head for a moment while I climb back onto the hurricane deck."

The buckskin tried to strike with its forefeet, but Longarm jumped sideways to grab the gelding's ear and wring it like a wet dishrag. Pain drove the horse into submission, and it shivered while Randy climbed back on, took up the rope, and shouted, "Turn him loose!"

The buckskin almost ran Longarm over before he could jump out of its path. The animal slammed into the corral poles with such force that one of them actually splintered. Bouncing off, the horse whirled and started bucking again.

Randy's nose was bleeding and his eyes appeared to be glazed, but he was mad. You could see it in the way he began to punish the buckskin just as he was being punished. For a few heart-stopping moments, it was a matter of whose will was going to prevail.

The buckskin quit first. It just tucked its black tail up a little, lowered its head, and spread its front legs wide while it gasped for breath and quivered.

"It's done," Randy said, gently nudging the animal forward and then reining it this way and that among the mustangs. "He's even got a good rein on him. He'd just forgotten what it was like to be ridden."

"I'm glad you're the one that took it upon yourself to show him," Longarm said. "Nice ride."

The rough outlaws that had gathered to surround the corral and watch were grinning, and even Matthew Killion himself had come over to watch his son bust the would-be bronc.

"Hell of a ride!" Matthew bellowed across the corral to his kid. "Damned good ride, son!"

Randy grinned. The only one who didn't look especially pleased was Clyde. His expression was grim, and Longarm thought he looked jealous before he turned and strode back to the saloon.

Even Desiree looked impressed with Randy. She was standing beside Killion, and Longarm thought she was just as pretty in the early morning sun as she'd been the previous day in the dimness of Killion's plush office. And although he'd been warned, Longarm found it impossible not to look at and admire her. Desiree had the looks of an actress and the body of a goddess.

She caught Longarm's eye and held it for a moment. He did not see an invitation in her look, but something seemed to have changed, for she did not seem to be regarding him as she might a bug either. Not the way she had the day before.

Longarm forced himself to turn and regard Randy and the buckskin. Randy rode over to his father and said, "This is a good animal. I stole him for ten dollars."

"He's kinda thin," Killion said, "but he's got a nice head, straight legs, and a deep chest."

"I expect he's fast," Randy said proudly. "And we can fatten him up."

"Why, sure we can," Killion said, slipping his arm around Desiree and dragging her young body up tight against his own.

Randy's smile died and he reined off toward the gate. George was there to open it, and the kid and his new horse rode through town, and were last seen galloping off in the direction of some low mountains.

"Follow 'em," Killion ordered one of his men, "just in case there is someone out there looking to even a score against me."

The man nodded and hurried to his horse. A few moments later, he was galloping hard out of Helldorado, following Randy's trail dust.

Longarm went over to Killion. "Your son promised us a good-bye breakfast if we helped him climb on that buckskin."

Killion nodded and appraised Longarm closely. "You and the Indian are hungry, huh?"

"We could stand to eat."

"You hurt one of my best men real bad last night."

"He didn't give me any choice," Longarm said. "Dean swore he was going to gut-shoot me."

"So I heard and so he tried."

Killion pushed Desiree away and Longarm stiffened a little, wondering if the man was going to try and kill him.

"I understand you were in the Yuma Territorial Prison for killing a man."

"That's right."

"How many cells do they have there?"

It was a trap question and Longarm, who had visited the prison on more than one occasion, had what he thought was the correct answer. "They're always building new cells. When I was there, the inmate population was about sixty, forty men and twenty women."

"Who was in charge?"

"Superintendent Frank Ingalls. I understand the bastard is still there cracking his whip."

"What kind of guns do the guards use?"

"They carry Winchesters in the towers, but it's the Lowell Battery Gun in Guard Tower Number Two that we mostly worried about. It could spray the whole damn compound and cut down anything that moved."

"And what was your worst punishment at Yuma?"

"I spend a month in the dark cell. It was hard."

"How big was it?"

Longarm sighed. "Mr. Killion, it was fifteen feet square and they kept me in a strap-iron cage that was placed in its center. You rarely saw the light of day, and you sat in your own slime. They gave you nothing but stale bread and cold river water."

"Where was it located?"

"In a cave bored out of solid rock along the south wall, right near the main cell block."

"All right," Killion said, apparently satisfied. "I guess that you know the Yuma prison better than any man ought. And as for Dean Holt, he had his bad whipping coming."

"Thanks."

"Why don't you stay," Killion suggested.

"Why? Are you going to buy anymore of our mustangs?"

"No, but you might find what I have in mind a lot more rewarding than mustanging."

"I'm listening."

"Are you good with that six-gun?"

"More than tolerable."

"Yeah," Killion said, "I'll just bet you are. How does a hundred dollars sound?"

"Like tall dollars."

Killion reached into his pocket and peeled off a hundred dollars. "You're hired."

"For what?" Longarm asked.

"Guarding Helldorado, and me."

Longarm clenched the money in his fist, knowing it was probably from some train, bank, or stagecoach robbery. "No offense, Mr. Killion, but you already appear to have an awful lot of guards. Why do you want another?"

"Because Dean was my toughest man and you proved yourself even tougher. I think you are probably as good with that six-gun as you are with your fists, and I'd like to have you on my side."

"Against who?"

"Anyone who opposes me or becomes my enemy."

Longarm took a deep breath and pretended to give the response all the serious consideration it warranted. This was exactly what he'd hoped would happen, but he did not want to appear too eager to accept. "When will more money be coming?"

Killion chuckled. "Sooner than it would if you kept mustanging."

"Yeah," Longarm said with a half smile. "I guess you have a good point."

"The girls are here for your pleasure. I'll pay you enough to have a daily taste of 'em, if that's what you like."

"I like." Longarm's eyes darted to Desiree's face.

"This one, however," Killion growled, reaching out to place his hand over the bulging fabric that covered her breast, "is *mine*."

"Understood, Boss."

"Good! I'm glad you're joining us. Now, send that Indian away."

"Why? He could use some—"

"Get rid of him and those mustangs," Killion ordered, "before I have the boys do it."

Longarm heard the threat and knew that this subject was not negotiable. "Yes, sir. Can't he at least eat first?"

Killion laughed. "Sure! He can eat all he wants, but then he's on his way. It's for his own good."

"I'll tell him that," Longarm said.

Killion started to escort Desiree back to his hotel, but he paused, then turned and said, "Randy wants you to teach him a few punches."

"He told me that."

"Then do it," Killion said with a cold smile as he left Longarm with a hundred dollars worth of stolen cash in his hand.

Chapter 13

Longarm walked George Two Ponies out to the corral, and then waited while the Paiute saddled his horse and got ready to depart Helldorado. Neither of them had said much while they'd shoveled a huge breakfast of steak and potatoes down their gullets. Longarm wasn't sure, but he thought that George was upset about leaving him without a friend in this outlaw town.

"I'll be fine, George. Stop worrying."

"If they kill you, I'll never get paid."

Longarm snorted. "Is that what you're upset about? Hell, I thought you were worried about my health!"

"Worried about hundred dollars too."

"All right," Longarm said, digging into his pockets. "Here's the ten dollars I got from Randy for that buckskin, plus half the money that I got from Killion. There's sixty dollars altogether, and if I survive this, you've got another forty coming."

George brightened considerably as he counted the money. Grinning, he said, "Longarm watch his back. Many bad peoples here. Bad spirits too."

"I know," Longarm said. "Here, I'll open the corral gate for you."

George mounted his horse and rode into the corral. He quickly drove the ponies out and had no difficulty in lining them north. Longarm suspected that the mustangs would head for their home range around Pyramid Lake with little urging. In fact, the real risk was in their running on ahead of George.

"He was a pretty good friend, huh?"

Longarm turned to see the kid. "Yeah. He was a good friend."

"How'd you meet him?"

"Mustanging."

"That's what you did after prison?"

"Among other things."

Longarm watched George and his mustangs disappear into the empty and barren Nevada hills. They would, he knew, go straight to the Carson River, where there was still some grass and lots of water. After a day, they would push on to Pyramid Lake, and he was pretty sure that George would buy his wife and children many nice things with that sixty dollars. It was probably more money that the Indian had made in the last six months.

"Dean says he's going to shoot you on sight," Randy said matter-of-factly.

"Thanks for the warning. Some men just have to learn the hard way. I expect that Dean is just one of those men."

"You need someone to watch your back."

"Who'd be willing to do that?"

"I might," Randy said.

Longarm looked at the kid. "And why would you want to help me?"

"I don't like Dean. He's a bully and he likes to hurt and even kill people."

"Have you killed yet, kid?"

"No," Randy said quietly, "not yet."

"But your father and brother have."

It wasn't a statement, and Longarm wanted to see what kind of reaction it would generate from the kid.

"My father has a lot of enemies. So does Clyde. I expect I have a few as well."

"But not like them," Longarm said pointedly. "Not the kind that want to kill you for murdering their friends and family."

Randy toed the earth and looked uncomfortable. "I'm a Killion."

"Yeah," Longarm said, "but you're also your own person."

Randy's brows knitted. "What are you trying to say?"

"I'm saying that you don't have to be like someone else just because you have their last name."

"Are you talking down my father and brother?" the kid asked, heat creeping into his voice.

"No," Longarm said quickly. "I'm not talking anyone down. I'm just saying we're all individuals with different ways of handling things. What might work for your father or brother might not set as well with you."

The kid tried to look angry. "What are you going to do now?" he finally said.

"I dunno. You father told me to give you a few tips about fighting."

Randy looked embarrassed. "I was sort of curious about how you were able to whip Dean without seeming to make much of a fuss over it. Up to then, I'd never seen or even heard of anyone whipping him."

"He's big, strong, and a bully," Longarm said. "He tried to bully me, but I called his bluff."

"Sure, but he wasn't bluffing, Custis. Dean is tough, and he'd have shot you through the gut if given half the chance."

"I knew that," Longarm said. "And that's why I didn't give him the chance. I hit him first, not after he'd knocked my teeth in. And when I hit him, I made the first blow count. I hit him as hard as I could where I knew it would do the most damage."

"You booted the hell out of him, too," Randy said.

"A man can break his hands up real easy on someone's head or even their face. If he breaks knuckles, he's in trouble because the pain is so bad he can't use that hand to fight. And if that is his gun hand, he's in double trouble. So you see, I used a boot not so much to hurt him as to avoid damaging my hands and putting myself at someone else's mercy."

"It makes sense," Randy said. "So you're saying the key to winning is to hit hard and hit first."

"That's right. When you throw that first punch, don't telegraph it either. Don't loop the punch and swing from the rafters or your bootstraps."

Longarm doubled up his fists and demonstrated. He moved closer to Randy and feigned two quick blows to the man's gut, then brought an uppercut up to the point of the kid's jaw that traveled less than six inches.

"Quick, hard, and short punches that start from close to the body and not somewhere out in thin air," he advised.

"And what happens if you get hit and go down?" Randy asked.

"Roll and keep rolling," Longarm said. "Get under

something and try to come out on the other side. And if you're pretty sure you're going to lose the fight, either punch for the throat or kick for the groin or grab ahold of a club and start swinging."

"You've got an answer for everything."

"No, I don't," Longarm admitted, "and I never pick fights the way that Dean picked one with me. I always try to avoid them, but if I have to fight, I fight to win and I don't worry about the Marquis of Queensberry's rules. In a barroom fight, anything goes, and I mean anything short of killing your opponent unless he is obviously trying to kill you."

"My father and Clyde are hard fighters," the kid said with no small measure of pride. "My father may look real long in the tooth, but he can whip any man in Helldorado with the possible exception of my brother, who'd never fight him."

"That's good," Longarm said. "I've seen sons whip their fathers, but it's a bad thing and there's never any good can come out of it, unless the father was one of those sonsabitches that just liked to beat his kids."

"My father never beat me, but he'll slap Desiree around a little if she gets mouthy."

"That'd be a shame," Longarm said, "as pretty as she is."

They talked for a little while longer, and then Randy told Longarm to pack his gear over to one of the hotels where a room was waiting.

"It ain't much, but the roof isn't burned out and the rain won't leak through it even in a bad storm."

"That's good enough for me."

Randy started to leave, but then he said, "You any good with explosives?"

Longarm blinked. "What makes you ask a question like that?"

"Just wondering," the kid said. "Are you?"

"I've handled dynamite before, and I know how to set and light a fuse."

"Good," Randy said. "My father will be happy to hear that."

"Randy?"

The kid turned, and Longarm sauntered over to him. "Is he thinking of a bank, or another train?"

Randy's jaw dropped. "What do you know about that?" he demanded.

"Nothing," Longarm said, "but it's easy enough to figure that your father isn't looking for me to use dynamite in the mines, now is he?"

Randy started to say something, then changed his mind and clamped his mouth shut before he walked away.

Longarm moved into a smaller hotel whose exterior rock walls were scorched and blackened. There were eight rooms on the second floor, and Longarm was given one already occupied by a tall, thin young outlaw named Eddie Tabor. Tabor had a jagged knife scar running diagonally across his face. His lower lip was badly scarred and twisted, making him look as if he'd just eaten something very, very bitter. He had thin brown hair and bad teeth. Even worse, he did not look you directly in the eye when you spoke to him, but sort of shifted his gaze from side to side.

"I hope you're not Dean's best friend and are planning on cutting my throat tonight," Longarm said, only half kidding as he spread his bedroll out and collapsed to take his ease.

"The only one you have to worry about is Dean," Tabor said. "The man didn't have a friend. He'd whipped most all of us and he had coming what you did to him."

"Glad to hear you say that."

"But he'll gun for you," Tabor warned. "I expect he's hanging out somewhere on a rooftop or in an alley waiting to get you in his gunsights. Best thing for you to do would be to kill him first."

"You mean just hunt him down?"

"Yeah, that's exactly what I mean."

"I'll give it some thought," Longarm said. "In the meantime, what does everyone do around here?"

"What are you driving at?"

"Well," Longarm said innocently, "I don't see much going on in the way of people making a living."

Tabor looked at him strangely. "We make a fine living. Hasn't Mr. Killion explained things?"

"Some," Longarm lied. "You know, about the trains and such, but I still expected people to keep busy."

"We do keep busy," Tabor explained. "There's always some of us out scouting up opportunities."

Longarm understood Tabor to mean that members of the gang were constantly searching for other banks, trains, stages, and individuals to rob, and then reporting their findings to Matthew Killion.

"How many jobs do you do a month?"

"Enough to live right," Tabor said. "We got good whiskey to drink, as much as we want, and we got some whores, though they're pretty worn out and not a damn bit lively unless you start to pinchin' 'em when they act too lazy."

"I see."

Tablor licked his lips and his eyes grew bright. "Some of them whores are from Mexico, and we've got some ex-prison girls too. Ones that have been in real trouble."

"*Nevada* prison girls, right?" Longarm asked, suddenly becoming nervous.

"Yeah, I expect. One named Lucy is from Arizona, though. Seems to me she was once in that same Yuma prison that they locked you up in. Hell, you might even know her!"

"I doubt it," Longarm said. "They kept the women and the men inmates as far away from each other as possible and we never hardly even saw one another. Most of the women in Yuma were as hard as nails."

"Lucy is hard, but she's also handsome. You don't pinch her, though. If you do that you're liable to get a knife shoved up your ass . . . if she don't first whack off your balls."

"I'll remember that," Longarm said.

"Good thing if you do." Tabor was leaving. "I don't like to hurt the girls anyway. And as for Lucy, she just sort of scares the piss outa me. I'd rather meet up with a cougar in a cave than Lucy in her bed."

"I'll stay away from her," Longarm vowed.

"Best you do," Tabor advised as he went out the door.

Chapter 14

That evening, Longarm went outside and headed across the street for the saloon. He was hungry and looking for a meal as well as a little sociable conversation. Not that Longarm had any illusions about making friends with anyone who'd ride with Killion's gang, because he was determined to bring the whole lot of them crashing down. But in his experience, men with whiskey in their bellies tended to open up and reveal secrets that they would never speak about when completely sober. With any luck, Longarm hoped he might even get one of Killion's men to spill his guts about that big Donner Pass train robbery.

Longarm was halfway across the street when a loud shout stopped him dead in his tracks.

"Hey, you big sonofabitch!"

Longarm's hand streaked for his six-gun even as he twisted around in the direction of the voice. A man was standing deep in the shadows between two buildings, and Longarm couldn't pinpoint his exact location until his six-gun stabbed muzzle flame.

A bullet struck Longarm in the ribs and its impact spun

him halfway around, probably saving his life. Longarm regained his balance and fired at the muzzle-flash. An instant later, he heard the man grunt. Before Longarm could get off another shot at his ambusher, he was gone, the sound of his boots pounding down the narrow corridor between two burned-out storefronts.

Longarm gripped his side and felt warm blood. He swore and limped after his man, but when he reached the spot where the man had fired, Longarm realized that he had too big a head start and would be impossible to overtake.

"What happened?" Randy asked, rushing up to join Longarm.

Longarm holstered his gun and pushed back his coat. "I was ambushed."

"By Dean?"

"He'd be my first guess." Longarm took a deep breath. The initial shock was wearing off to be replaced by a deep, throbbing pain in his side. "I managed to return fire and I'm pretty sure that Dean took a bullet."

"And he just opened fire on you from ambush?"

"That's right."

"We'll find him," Randy vowed, his eyes dropping to Longarm's side. "How bad are you hurt?"

"I might have broken a rib," Longarm said through gritted teeth. "I dunno."

"We'll take you over to see Lucy."

"What for? Isn't she the ex-convict from Yuma?"

"That's right, and she's also the best in Helldorado when it comes to patching a man up. Besides," Randy said, "you might even know her from the days when you and she were both inmates down in the Arizona Territory."

"Not likely," Longarm said quickly. "And I'd just as soon let the doctorin' wait until I find Dean before he tries to ambush me again."

"Maybe you killed him."

"I don't think so," Longarm said. "He was running pretty hard when he took off."

"There's no place to run in Helldorado," Randy said confidently. "Let's go find Lucy and have her take care of the damage. There sure isn't any sense in standing here jawing while you bleed to death."

That made good sense to Longarm, so he followed Randy back across the street. Matthew and Clyde Killion were waiting to meet them, and it seemed everyone in Helldorado had gathered around to learn about the cause of the gunfire.

"What happened?" Matthew demanded, big arms folded across his chest and face hard with anger.

Randy pulled up before his father and said, "Custis was ambushed."

"By who?" Killion addressed his question to Longarm.

"I don't know," Longarm admitted. "Someone called out and I turned and was shot. I fired back, and I'm almost certain I hit the man who tried to cut me down."

"Was it Dean Holt?"

Before Longarm could answer, Clyde pushed forward and interrupted. "Pa, it couldn't have been Dean. Hell, you saw him! Dean was so beat up he could barely walk."

But Killion shook his head with disagreement. "Son, when a man is fueled by hatred, he has the power to do amazing things. Hatred fires a man like no other emotion."

"Yes, sir."

"Find Dean. If he's wounded and layin' up, drag him to me kicking and screaming."

"Yes, sir," Clyde said, obviously not pleased with the order but not ready to argue about it either.

"Randy, take our friend Custis over to see Lucy," Killion said. "She'll fix him up."

"We were just on our way over to see her."

"You didn't take lead in the gut, did you?" Killion asked, looking closely at the blood seeping from Longarm's side.

"No, sir," Longarm replied. "I've just been grazed. Maybe the slug splintered a rib. I don't know, but it feels like I've just had a burning branding iron slapped to my hide."

"Well," Killion promised, "if Dean turns up shot, he's gonna wish you'd already put him out of his misery."

Killion turned slightly, and his voice grew loud as he spoke to every man in Helldorado. "Boys, one rule that I won't stand to be broken is that we don't kill each other. I've said this before, but I'll say it again. If there is hatred between you, settle it with your fists. When one man can't rise, the fight is over. You shake hands and bury the hatchet."

Killion paused, his eyes raking the Helldorado outlaws. "But boys, if one of you uses a gun or a knife against another, you'll not live long to regret it."

Longarm didn't know what Killion had in mind for Dean, and the thought occurred to him that Killion might even torture the wounded outlaw. Either way, Longarm had a strong suspicion that Dean's punishment wasn't going to be pleasant to watch. On the other hand, it was hard to feel sorry for the ambusher. Sympathy was wasted on his kind because such men sought no quarter

142

and would kill you without a moment's hesitation.

"Custis, come along," Randy said impatiently. "Let's find Lucy before you bleed to death."

"Sounds like the thing to do."

They found Lucy tipped back in a saloon chair with her high-heeled shoes resting on a faro table as she examined the runs in her black silk stockings. She was a tall woman, willowy, with long, shapely legs. Her straight black hair was shoulder length, and she obviously took pride in it because it gleamed as the result of heavy brushing. Lucy's still-attractive face showed the inevitable telltale signs of hard living, although she could not have been over thirty. There were dark smudges around her eyes, and her fingernails were bitten to the quick. Longarm's first impressions were generally correct, and this one told him that Lucy was high-strung, tough, and smart.

"I heard the shooting," Lucy said, staring at Longarm and his bloody shirt. "I guess that Dean went and plugged you, huh, big fella?"

"I think it was him," Longarm said heavily, "although I can't be sure."

"Who else would do it given that everyone knows what will happen to them if they're caught? A man would have to be crazed with hatred to do such a foolish thing in Helldorado."

"Well," Longarm said, "why don't you take a look at the damage and we can speculate as to who done it later."

"Sure," Lucy said, dropping her feet to the floor. "Come on over here and pull off your coat and your shirt."

Longarm needed Randy's assistance, and when he was

finished removing the clothing, sweat had beaded on his forehead. Lucy had not even gotten out of her chair, and Longarm sidled up to her so that the woman could make her examination.

"How bad is it?" he asked.

"Well," she said, leaning forward with a bar towel and dabbing the blood away, "it's bad enough to hurt."

"I already *knew* that," Longarm said with exasperation. "Is the rib damaged?"

"It appears to be." Lucy pressed the bar towel down harder and fingered the wound. "But I don't think it's broken. Another fraction of an inch and it would have been a real mess. You're a pretty lucky man."

"Yeah," Longarm said drily.

Lucy looked over at several of the other girls. "Myra, Betty, bring me some hot water and clean linen for bandages. And bring me a needle and thread. This needs to be sewn up or he'll keep leaking."

Lucy finally came out of her chair and said, "Why don't you just sit down before you pass out."

"I'm not going to pass out."

"Sure, you're just like all the other brave bastards in Helldorado. Too damned tough to be smart. You need whiskey for your pain and you look like death warmed over."

"You're no prize yourself," Longarm told the woman. "How long do you go without sleep?"

"Depends on how much business I'm doing and how horny the men are on any particular day. In this shit-hole town, there isn't much for any of us to do but drink and screw. Helldorado is a real—"

"Shut up, Lucy," Randy ordered in a stern voice.

"Your wagging tongue is going to get you in real deep trouble one of these days."

"It already has, kid."

A bottle arrived, and Longarm gulped down several long slugs, feeling better almost immediately as Randy and Lucy glared at each other.

Finally, Lucy managed a cold smile. "If I wasn't wanted by the law, kid, why else do you think I'd stay in Helldorado? Hell, Randy, wake up! Everyone in this miserable town is bound for a sorry end. If you don't believe that you're only fooling yourself."

"Lucy, shut up and doctor Custis!" Randy snapped. "I swear you talk too damned much."

Lucy's lips tightened in a hard line, and she was quiet until the hot water, needle, thread, and bandages arrived and were placed on the poker table. Then she looked at Longarm and said, "I need you back on your feet until this is over."

Longarm stood again, and was surprised to discover that his legs felt weak and he was dizzy. The whiskey was hitting him hard, but he took another stiff drink before he laced his fingers behind his back and clenched his teeth as Lucy went to work on his torn flesh with her needle and thread. To Longarm's relief, the suturing didn't increase his pain. The sewing went slowly, but when it was finally done, Lucy quickly and expertly bandaged the wound, wrapping Longarm's entire torso.

"I'm done," Lucy said, "so you can relax and get good and drunk. Your head will feel worse for it tomorrow morning, but you'll sleep tonight."

Longarm sat and reached for the bottle. He wasn't going to get drunk, but he was going to take a little more painkiller and then hobble back to his room and call it a night. He had no more than picked up the bottle, however, when he heard a big commotion outside.

"What do you suppose is going on?" Longarm asked no one in particular.

"I think they've already found Dean," Randy said, looking very grim as he went to the door and peered outside. "Yep," he called back. "They got him."

"Lucy, what is Matthew Killion going to do to Dean?"

"I don't exactly know," Lucy confessed, taking a pull on Longarm's bottle, "but I expect that he'll die slowly."

Longarm sucked in a deep breath. He had no love or sympathy for Dean, but neither could he stand idly by while the man was systematically tortured.

Dean howled in pain, and Longarm heard loud voices and a great deal of cursing before Matthew and Clyde Killion burst into the saloon, followed by Dean and most of the town's outlaws.

All eyes turned to Longarm, and Killion shouted, "He's been shot, all right. You winged him in the forearm and we caught him trying to steal one of our horses and escape."

"It was my own damned horse!" Dean squalled. "Mister Killion, I swear I'd never steal anything from you!"

Killion hauled up short and spun around to hit Dean. The wounded outlaw's legs buckled and he had to be supported. Killion stepped forward and hauled the man up to his toes.

"Dean, you know the rules in Helldorado. You know I won't stand for one of us killing another. You broke that rule and you were trying to get out before you got caught."

Dean's head wobbled loosely on his big shoulders. His

face, already a mess from the beating that he'd taken from Longarm, was now bleeding again, probably the result of the struggle it had taken to capture and deliver him to this place.

"Just let me go," Dean begged. "I been loyal to you, Mr. Killion! I killed men for you and I—"

Killion hit him again, this time crushing Dean's lips to pulp and dropping him to the floor. Longarm came to his feet. His head was swimming and he felt reckless. "He's no dog," Longarm said. "So don't beat him like one."

Killion spun around, eyes slitting. "What did you say?"

"I said he's not a dog," Longarm answered evenly. "He's a man."

"He's a horse thief and an ambusher," Killion said, his voice shaking with rage. "And furthermore, he works for me and I make the rules in this town. So sit down, and if you say another word, I'll finish what Dean could not. Do I make that very clear?"

Longarm felt the icy finger of death reaching out to tap him on the shoulder. Matthew Killion was not bluffing and Longarm, despite the revulsion he felt, knew that he would forfeit his life if he said another word.

Randy knew it too because he leaned forward and whispered, "Just shut up."

Longarm picked up his bottle and turned to Lucy. "Thank you for the fine doctoring job, Miss Lucy. Now, if you'll all excuse me, I need some fresh air."

Longarm limped past Killion, their eyes locking for a moment. No one dared to stop Longarm as he found the door and passed outside, bottle clenched in his big hand. He wasn't ready to die for a man like Dean Holt, but he

147

surc wasn't ready to watch the man suffer either.

Holt's first scream was the loudest, and it sent a chill all the way down Longarm's spine. The second scream was that of a dying animal, and Longarm was jerked up short in his tracks. He took a long drink and slowly pivoted around, a man caught between the dictates of his conscience and his own tenuous mortality. He dropped the bottle and reached for his six-gun, then started back toward the saloon. He was almost at the door when two gunshots erupted from inside.

"God damn you, Randy!" Killion shouted, his voice booming through the open doorway. "I wasn't finished with him yet!"

"Yes, you were, Pa," was Randy's reply a moment before he came stumbling out of the saloon to nearly collide with Longarm.

Their eyes met and held. Then Randy said, "I've killed a man now, Custis. I just shot Dean."

There was such a terrible sadness in the kid's expression that Longarm holstered his own six-gun and then he took Randy's gun and shoved it behind his belt.

"You didn't kill that man, your father did," Longarm said, taking Randy's arm and leading him away. "Is there another saloon where we can get drunk?"

"I got a bottle of fine Kentucky mash whiskey up in my room," Randy said. "Good stuff that I've been saving for a special occasion."

"Well," Longarm said, "this isn't a special occasion, but we need to drink that whiskey anyway and to talk."

"About what?" Randy asked, his expression dull with shock.

"About you and this town and the Donner Pass train robbery and a bunch of other things."

148

Randy came to a sudden halt. "What do you know about that train robbery?"

Longarm chose his words carefully for he was not about to give his true identity away to Matthew Killion's son, not yet at least.

"Men talk. Everyone in Nevada knows it was your father's gang that robbed that train."

"People can talk forever, but without proof . . ."

"Yeah," Longarm said, "without proof it's all just smoke, ain't it, kid."

"That's right."

They walked up the street to another hotel, and then they climbed the stairs to Randy's room. It was spartan, but clean, and Longarm was not really surprised to see that there were a goodly number of books. Shakespeare and other poets, mostly, but also some philosophy books and, amazing for a place like this, a copy of the Holy Bible.

Longarm went over and picked the bible up while Randy found his good Kentucky mash. Longarm opened the cover and saw that the bible had been inscribed and it read: *To Randy from Lupe, walk with Him always.*

"Put that down!" Randy ordered.

Longarm set the bible down. "What happened to Señora Sanchez?"

Randy blinked with surprise. "How did you know about her?"

"People talk."

Randy started to say something, but changed his mind. He clamped his mouth shut and found two clean water glasses. He filled them to the brim, and his hand was shaking so badly when he picked them up and extended one to Longarm that he spilled some whiskey.

"Who are you?" Randy whispered.

"To a better life," Longarm said, ignoring the question as he raised his glass. "And to justice and a fresh start."

Randy drank deeply and closed his eyes. Longarm watched as color flooded back into the kid's face.

"You *didn't* kill that man," Longarm said gently. "Dean Holt was already a dead man. We all knew that. Your father killed him and you just put the man out of his misery. What you did was a kind and a merciful thing, Randy."

Randy's eyes popped open. "Do you mean that?"

"Yes, I do."

"My father has a good side," Randy said. "He's always been good to Clyde and me. He's never beat us and he's always given us whatever we needed."

"Except a respect for the law and for the lives of others," Longarm said.

Randy bristled. "Maybe it looks that way to you, Custis, but he's good to people who show him loyalty."

"I'm not impressed. What right does your father have to judge and then execute someone like Dean?"

"The man broke our rules! Without that rule against killing each other, there would be a lot more bloodshed. It's a rule that had to be made."

Longarm shook his head. "I just have a hard time with someone who sets himself up with the power to give or take life. It's not right and I think you know it."

Randy drank quickly. His eyes blinked like things trapped inside a cage. "When are you going to tell me who you *really* are?"

"When the time is right."

Randy heaved a deep sigh. "Why don't we both just shut up and get roaring drunk!"

"Okay," Longarm said, knowing the kid would tell him everything he needed to know about the Killion gang long before the night was over.

Chapter 15

Early the next morning, Longarm rolled stiffly off of a couch and shuffled over to look out through Randy's hotel window. To the east, he could see the first faint glow of sunrise. Longarm wished he had a cup of coffee. He felt awful because both his head and his side throbbed with pain. One because of a bullet, the other because of the whiskey, and he couldn't decide which one was troubling him the most.

Longarm had an important decision to make and it had to be made quickly. During the early morning hours, Randy had drunkenly confessed that his father's gang had robbed the Union Pacific up on Donner Pass and gotten away with nearly ten thousand dollars. And while Randy had not participated in that daring train robbery, he had been told by Clyde that he would be expected to ride with the Killion gang on their upcoming raid against the Bank of Reno located on South Virginia Street. Longarm knew the bank well, for it was Reno's biggest and he had cashed many a government travel check there. Randy had not been privy to any of the details of the upcoming robbery, not even the exact day it would occur. But Longarm had no doubt that it would occur, and that it would be successful unless he did something to thwart the Killion gang.

Even more troubling for the kid had been Señora Lupe Sanchez's sudden and mysterious departure from Helldorado. She had simply vanished without a good-bye or an explanation to Randy.

"I don't know if she just ran away to escape my father or . . . or what," Randy had sadly confessed.

Longarm had not had the heart to tell the kid that, in his opinion, Matthew Killion had probably ordered that Lupe Sanchez be killed and her body disposed of someplace where it would never be found.

"Maybe," Longarm had told the anguished and drunken young man, "if you can figure out some way to get us out of Helldorado for a few days, we can find the *señora.*"

"How?"

Longarm, frankly, wasn't sure, but he thought it was worth a try. It was obvious that Killion's former mistress had become like a mother to Randy. If she were found alive, Longarm felt sure that she would be able to talk Randy into betraying his father and his brother. She was, Longarm believed, the only one who had enough influence on Randy to save him from eventually making mistakes that would bring him to the gallows or at least earn him a long prison sentence.

"Randy," Longarm now said, making the decision that they had to get out of Helldorado for a day or two and attempt to find Lupe Sanchez. "Wake up, it's time to ride."

Randy wasn't easy to awaken, and when he finally managed to open his eyes, they were bloodshot.

Longarm shook the kid even harder. "We've got to go look for Señora Sanchez."

Randy moaned. "I'm afraid that she's . . . she's long dead, Custis."

"Well, we don't know that for certain, do we? And until we find out for sure, we have to at least try to find her. Now come on and let's get our horses and get out of here before anyone else awakens."

Randy sat up. His face was pale and puffy. It looked like the belly of a dead carp. Longarm dragged the kid to his feet. "You need to write a note to your father explaining that we got drunk and decided to ride up to the Comstock Lode and continue our celebration."

"Pa will kill us."

"No, he won't," Longarm said, dragging the kid to a table where a pencil and pad of paper were waiting. "Now write him a note saying we'll be back in a couple of days."

"All right," Randy said, "but he's going to be madder than hell that I didn't get permission first."

"Life is full of disappointments," Longarm snapped.

"Where are we *really* going?"

"I don't know," Longarm admitted. "That will depend on where you think Señora Sanchez would go to hide."

"And if she's dead?"

"Then you're going to have to help me bring her killers to justice."

Randy's jaw dropped. "You're a lawman! Jezus! I could have you drawn and quartered! If my father or brother—"

Longarm reached out and grabbed Randy by the front of his shirt and shook him until his teeth rattled. "Listen, damn you!" he swore. "We're going to find out if your father had Señora Sanchez murdered."

Longarm pushed Randy back on his heels. "Kid, I'm going to nail your father and this whole damn rotten bunch because they're a pack of thieves and murderers. And frankly, if you try to stop me, a lot of blood is going to flow, yours, mine, and for damn sure your father and brother's."

Randy was sober now and shaking his head. "Custis, I just can't betray my father and brother."

Longarm resisted the urge to grab the kid and shake some sense into him. Instead, he knelt at Randy's side, ignored the pain in his ribs, and said, "What if your father callously ordered Señora Sanchez's death? Are you just going to forgive him? Allow him to murder and steal and say it's all right because you are the same blood?"

Longarm paused for a moment and then he continued. "And what about Clyde? He's a bully and a killer. Did you know that a trainman up on Donner Pass was pistol-whipped so viciously that he might even die? That he can't ever work again to support his family and that his life is forever ruined?"

A sob escaped Randy's throat. He turned away from Longarm and staggered over to sit back down on his bed. Longarm wanted to ease up on Randy, but he knew that was the wrong thing to do. He had the kid frightened, confused, and uncertain. In time, Longarm was certain that Randy would do the right thing, especially if he found out that Lupe Sanchez had come to a tragic end because she had known too much about Matthew Killion.

"Let's go," Longarm demanded impatiently. "We're running out of time."

"I'm not going," Randy said, staring down between his feet.

Longarm grabbed Randy and hauled him erect. "You either go now, or I'm going to march over to arrest your father and let the chips fall where they may."

"Custis, if you try that, you're a dead man as sure as the sun is rising."

"You're probably right, but I'll take your father, your brother, and a whole lot more with me."

Randy must have believed him because he swallowed drily, then slowly nodded his head. "All right, let's go see if we can find Lupe."

"Now you're making sense," Longarm said with a wide grin. "Any ideas where we can start looking?"

"A couple."

"Good. Let's get out of here before someone sees us and starts asking questions."

"Someone will anyway," Randy said as he quickly began to dress. "Pa's put a guard out by the road into Helldorado. He's going to question us."

"Then you'd better have some answers for him," Longarm said, "because we're leaving."

"And if my answers aren't good enough?"

"Then the guard might contract lead poisoning," Longarm said, pulling on his own shirt and coat and fighting back the pain from his bullet wound.

They had no trouble getting their horses saddled even though the sun had floated off the horizon and was blazing warmth across the sage-covered hills. The blue-green pinyon and juniper pine were damp with dew and steaming. About twenty-five miles to the west, the Sierra Nevadas stood like a line of tall medieval soldiers, helmets glistening with snow. It was an extraordinarily beautiful morning and, had it not been for the possibility that he might have to kill a guard, Longarm would have greatly enjoyed this sojourn.

"There he is," Randy said, pointing to a man who rode out from a gully and approached them with a rifle cradled across the fork of his saddle.

"Is he reasonable?" Longarm asked.

"When he's sober," Randy said.

"Make him a believer," Longarm warned. "We need to act a little drunk ourselves."

"Hello there!" Randy called to the approaching guard with a loose grin and then a dry cackle. "Stayin' warm this morning, Gil? Or are you freezin' your ass off?"

Gil was a nondescript fellow, all bundled up in winter clothing and wearing heavy leather gloves on his hands.

"I damn near froze last night! Gonna be relieved in about an hour and the first thing I'm going to do is to find me a whore and warm myself up in her bed."

Randy forced a sick smile. "Me and Custis been drinkin' and whorin' all night. We plumb wore 'em all out, Gil!"

"The hell you say," Gil exclaimed, shaking his head. "Where are you fellas headed?"

"Virginia City, by gawd!"

Gil's smile slipped. "Mr. Killion didn't say anything about anyone leaving Helldorado this morning."

"We're going to have us a high old time, Gil. My father won't care."

Gil frowned. "I don't think you ought to do that without asking him first."

"He won't mind," Randy said, his pathetic smile fading. "Now, just don't give me any trouble, Gil."

"But it's my ass if your father finds out you're gone and he didn't want you to. You know that we're riding north to hit that Reno bank Friday morning."

"We're gonna be back a day before that," Randy said, prodding his new buckskin forward. "This horse needs riding and I need to see some new whores."

"Yeah, but . . ."

"Out of the way, Gil," Longarm said quietly. "We're getting thirstier by the minute."

Gil made a feeble attempt to block their path, but Longarm reined his horse past the man, and then they were trotting down the cold road toward the Comstock Lode.

"You better not be the cause of me getting on Mr. Killion's shit list!" Gil shouted. "You'd better not, Randy!"

Randy didn't respond. He just kept riding, and so did Longarm. "See," Longarm finally said cheerfully, "no problem. And now we know exactly when your father and his gang plan to rob the Bank of Reno."

"So you can lay a trap and ambush them?"

"No," Longarm said, "so we can lay a trap and catch them by surprise and make our arrests before anyone else gets killed or hurt."

"They'll *never* surrender."

"Then they'll die," Longarm said heavily. "It's their call, but I promise you that we'll give them a choice. That's the best that they can hope for, kid."

Randy swallowed and stared straight ahead as they rode on into the cold morning to learn if Señora Lupe Sanchez was dead or alive.

Chapter 16

"All right, Randy," Longarm said, "assuming that Señora Sanchez is still alive, where do you think she might have gone after leaving Helldorado?"

"There's a town called Mormon Station just southwest of Carson City."

"I know it well," Longarm said. "The town was cursed when Brigham Young called his flock back to the Utah Territory and forced them to practically give away their land."

"That's right," Randy said. "Lupe's son lives and works there. His name is Arturo and he's a few years older than I am."

"Wouldn't that be the first place anyone would look for Lupe?"

"Sure," Randy admitted, "but Arturo would never tell anyone what he knew. But he trusts me and he'll tell us if she's dead or alive."

"So how come Arturo didn't come to Helldorado and help his mother?"

"What could he have done other than gotten himself

159

killed?" Randy asked. "My father would never brook any interference."

"And Lupe allowed herself to be shut off from her son?"

"Every few months she would go to visit Arturo, his wife, and two children. I would always accompany her and stay at their place. We had good times there."

Longarm chewed on that for a few minutes. "And did it ever occur to you just to stay in Mormon Station?"

"Sure!" Randy lowered his voice. "I often thought about staying. There's a freighting road nearby that crosses over the Sierras that I could have worked on as a mule skinner. There are plenty of ranch jobs in that Carson Valley."

"Then why didn't you stay?"

"Lupe would talk me out of it."

Longarm blinked with surprise. "She talked you out of leaving Helldorado? I don't understand."

"She . . ." Randy had to clear his voice. "She loved my father. You see, he is capable of being kind and generous. The first time that they met, my father whipped two bullies who had been harassing Lupe and making her life miserable. Then, he bought Lupe roses and courted her for two years, not once crossing the bounds of a gentleman."

"While he had his whores to play with at night," Longarm said, "and his get-rich-quick schemes designed to fleece the innocent and trusting."

"Lupe had an old dog," Randy said, not listening but trying desperately hard to defend his father. "I saw my father pick it up after it had been run over by a wagon and gallop twenty miles to get it to a doctor and then

160

pay him a hundred dollars for saving that dog's life and making Lupe happy again."

Longarm was not greatly impressed. "All right, so he would do anything for the *señora*. That's easy enough to understand because I've heard she was not only beautiful, but also a fine woman."

"She is a saint," Randy confessed. "She also has a fine education. When my father finally talked her into moving to Helldorado, she brought boxes and boxes of books. They're the ones you saw in my room last night. Lupe can recite poetry by the hour."

"I still can't understand what she saw in your father."

"And I doubt that you ever will," Randy said. "He's changed a great deal in the last five years, and not for the better. Lupe loved my father, and he was true to her until a couple of years ago. That's what hurt her the most. That, and the killing."

"Did she talk to you about leaving?"

"Oh, yes! But even as she would talk about it, she continued to hold out hope for my father. She would read the Bible and pray for him. I never saw a woman so prayerful as Lupe. She would ask me to pray for him too. And also for my brother."

"What did Clyde think of Lupe?"

"He hated her," Randy admitted. "He thought she was poison. Clyde and I used to argue, and then Clyde would whip me when I defended Lupe."

"So what finally happened?"

Randy expelled a deep breath. "Clyde got worse, and finally he whipped me so badly that I had to be taken to Carson City and looked after by the doctors. My mother . . . I mean Lupe, she almost killed Clyde herself. She would have if one of the Ten Commandments hadn't forbidden her to kill. Anyway, she confronted my father and demanded that he punish Clyde with a bullwhip."

"But your father refused?"

"You guessed it," Randy said. "My brother was full-grown and he said he'd rather go down with a smoking gun in his hand than be horsewhipped. That was it. My father wasn't willing to gun down Clyde, and so Lupe must have figured that she'd had enough."

It made sense to Longarm, and he turned his thoughts to more immediate and pressing concerns. "Randy, are you any good with that six-gun?"

"I am *very* good with a six-gun."

"Show me."

"Oh, no," Randy said wagging his aching head, "not this morning. I'm shaky and couldn't hit anything."

"Try," Longarm urged. "Draw and fire at that tree over yonder. It's important that I see exactly what you can do."

It was a dead pinyon pine with withered branches jutting out from its trunk. Randy reined his buckskin up sharply and took another deep breath. "You aren't going to be impressed," he said. "Not given the horrible way I feel."

"Just see if you can hit the tree."

Randy drew and fired in one smooth motion. It wasn't as fast as Longarm's draw, but given the kid's pathetic condition, Randy did remarkably well, and managed to get three bullets into the tree before the buckskin lowered its head and went to bucking. Randy's gun spilled from his hand and he grabbed for leather. It was all he could do to hang on as the buckskin kicked its heels at the rising sun and almost pitched Randy into the sage.

"Dammit!" Randy hollered, finally dragging the gelding's head up and getting the animal under control. "I'm in no mood for this kind of shit! Not in my half-dead condition!"

Longarm had to laugh at the poor kid's misery even though it hurt his own bandaged ribs. He dismounted and retrieved Randy's six-gun, and then he walked over to the pinyon and studied the bullet holes.

"Damn good shooting by anyone, drunk or sober," was his pronouncement. "You've practiced a lot, haven't you."

"Yeah," Randy confessed. "I knew right from the start that I'd never be as big or as strong as my brother and that he'd always kick my butt. There came a time when I learned that Mister Colt would have to be my equalizer."

"As it is for a lot of men," Longarm said. "And I suspect that's what finally kept you from getting your head beat in by Clyde."

"Maybe."

Longarm gave the kid back his gun. "I just hope that Lupe Sanchez is still alive. She sounds like the kind of woman I'd like to meet."

"You won't charm her," Randy warned. "She's too Christian a woman to fall for the likes of you."

"She fell for your father."

"And has regretted it ever since," Randy said, his eyes on the distant mountains.

They arrived at Arturo Sanchez's little farm late that afternoon, and it was just as Randy had described. Arturo raised a few head of cattle, traded horses, and had a truck garden and a big chicken pen. Randy had said that Arturo

163

also worked for some of the neighboring ranches during haying season, and did odd jobs in town when someone was sick, injured, or just needed an extra hand.

Arturo was a handsome man in his early twenties, with a soft, round wife named Monica who giggled a lot and two of the cutest little daughters a man could ever hope to love.

"Come inside," Arturo said, leaving the wagon wheel he had been repairing. "The wind, she is cold and I have some tequila."

Even the mere mention of a drink caused Randy to blanch and shake his head vigorously.

"The hair of the dog," Longarm told the kid from Helldorado. "A few nips will perk you up."

"No, thanks. You've never tasted Arturo's tequila, but I have."

Randy's remark was made only partially in jest, and it caused Arturo to laugh and his wife to giggle. They went inside a small two-room cabin, and there was a fire burning in the hearth and Monica Sanchez had a pot of beans and beef bubbling.

"You're gonna love her cooking," Randy promised.

Randy's prediction was right on the mark, and Longarm ate until he was ready to burst. Besides the beans and beef, there were hot corn bread muffins with honey, and then later, coffee and even a delicious spice cake.

The meal and the company should have resulted in a happy occasion, but it did not. Arturo and Randy tried to sound as if they were having fun, but Longarm could sense that there was a tension between them and that the two young men were eager to talk about Lupe Sanchez.

164

"Let me show you the new mule that I bought to pull the plow for Monica's garden next spring," Arturo suggested a short time later.

Longarm allowed as how that would be interesting, and he tagged along behind the two men as they walked to the barn. It was a small barn and the mule was in poor condition and unsound.

"What is wrong with him?" Randy asked.

"He was beaten too much and starved," Arturo said. "He went lame after being forced to pull too big a load up the mountain too often, eh?"

"Will he recover?"

The Mexican shrugged. "I paid only five dollars for him. With rest this winter, and with lots of food and even the prayers of my family, who knows? It is up to God, eh?"

"Yes," Randy said, "it is up to him. I hope that he makes your mule well, Arturo."

"Me too," the Mexican said. He toed the earth. "Have you come to ask about Mother?"

"I have."

"After all these months? Why?"

Randy shifted his weight and jammed his hands into his pockets. "I longed to know about her from the moment she disappeared. I agonized to come here, but I was afraid it would cause you trouble. And I thought that, if I didn't come, maybe Lupe would be better off and so would you."

Arturo accepted this. "And what do you want to know?"

"Is she alive?" His voice held a desperate note that no one could have failed to miss.

Arturo walked around the mule so that it was between

165

them, and he scratched the animal's large ears. "Do you swear secrecy?"

"Of course! On my life, Arturo!"

The farmer turned to regard Longarm, although he was still speaking to Randy. "And what of this tall friend with the bullet wound in his side? Why should I trust a stranger?"

"Because," Longarm said, digging into his pocket and showing the Mexican his United States marshal's badge, "I'm a federal lawman."

If Arturo was surprised, Randy was astonished. "My God! You've been carrying that on your person in Helldorado!"

"No one was going to take it off me unless they killed me first," Longarm said, "and if they did that, why should I care anymore?"

"You're crazy," Randy said.

"You're a marshal," Arturo said. "Then you should hear what I have to say about this evil thing that happened to my mother."

"I'm listening."

"She ran away from Helldorado and they had chased her almost to this place before the darkness fell. When I found her in this barn, she had been shot."

"No!" Randy wailed.

Tears seeped from Arturo's eyes. "It is true. My mother was shot by two of your father's men."

"How do you know this?"

"Because she told me who they were."

"Their names!" Randy choked.

"You do not want to—"

Randy shouted, "Dammit, their names!"

"One was named Dean. The other was your brother."

166

"Is the *señora* still alive?" Longarm asked.

"*Sí*," Arturo said after a moment's hesitation. "She lives!"

Joy sprang back into Randy's eyes. "Thank God!" he cried. "Where is she? I want to see her!"

"No," Arturo said. "She has gone away."

"But where?"

"To California. To Sonora, where there are many of our Mexican people. It is just over the mountains, and I have already gone to visit her twice. She is going to be well soon, but she will never return to Nevada."

Randy bowed his head and Longarm thought the kid was crying again, until he realized that Randy was offering a prayer of thanks.

Before Longarm went to bed that night, Monica changed his bandages and cleaned his wound. "It's not a very pretty thing for you to see," he said in the way of an apology.

"You will soon heal, *señor*."

"That's good to hear," Longarm said, speaking directly to Randy. "There's a lot of work to be done in the next few days."

"That's right," Randy said, his face set with determination. "There is."

That was all that Longarm wanted to hear, and later that night he slept better than he had in months. It was almost nine o'clock the next morning when one of Arturo's children finally forgot to be silent and awakened him with laughter.

Longarm smiled. He realized that to awaken to the laughter of a child was a blessing.

"Breakfast, Señor Long?" Monica asked.

"I apologize for sleeping so late," Longarm said. "I expect the household has been up for hours, everyone creeping around and trying not to make a sound and wake me."

"No," she said, "everyone noisy, but you snore so loud you cannot hear us."

Longarm chuckled at that, and took his place at Monica's table. There were eggs, ham, and flapjacks, of which he ate piles. "I swear that if I had regular cooking like this, I'd be as big as a horse."

Monica beamed, her face round and gentle as she went to see to her children.

Longarm finished his breakfast, and went outside to discover that Randy's buckskin and his own ugly black gelding were saddled and bridled.

"We're leaving now?" Longarm asked with surprise.

"I've got scores to settle."

"Whoa up there," Longarm said. "This is my kind of game and we're playing by my rules."

"What does that mean?"

"It means that we're going to bring your father's gang to justice without a bunch of good men getting killed, us being among 'em. Is that clear?"

"No."

"It will become so as we ride," Longarm said, grunting with pain as he climbed stiffly into his saddle.

"Side hurts pretty bad, huh?" Randy asked.

"It's more of a bother. How is your head today?"

"Clear and seeing things for the way they are, thank you," Randy said with a smile.

"Good," Longarm said, liking the spark and determination he was witnessing in the kid.

They said a hurried good-bye to the Sanchez family,

and rode away with prayers for their safety ringing in their ears.

"Nice family," Longarm said, looking back and waving.

"Arturo said that my father came here not too long ago."

"He did?"

"That's right," Randy answered. He turned to look at Longarm. "And do you know what else Arturo said?"

"No."

"My father threatened to kill the lot of them if Lupe ever testified or named him as the leader of that train robbery."

"I see."

Randy's voice shook with anger. "Can you believe that! My father threatened to kill the children!"

"I imagine that Arturo is pretty scared."

"Damn right," Randy said. "Clyde and my father lashed him to a post in the barn and used a whip on him until he bled. When he still wouldn't tell them where Lupe had gone, they nearly went after Monica and the kids, but he begged them to leave his family alone, and finally they did."

"They could have a change of heart and return to Arturo's homestead and carry out that threat."

"I know that," Randy said. "And that's why I'm going to do whatever it takes to make sure that they never hurt anyone again."

"We're going to Reno," Longarm told the kid. "We're going to see the marshal there and tell him about that upcoming bank robbery."

"But why can't we just tell the authorities that we have evidence and let them take a ride into Helldorado? Hell,

Custis, they could even drag the United States Army into it."

"And a lot of good soldiers would be killed. No," Longarm said, "we'll catch them in the act of robbery so that there can be no doubt as to their guilt."

"Whatever you say," Randy replied.

"Which brings me to another question," Longarm added. "Do you know where your father has stashed that Donner Pass train robbery money?"

"He's spent a lot of it," Randy said. "Those Helldorado girls and all that whiskey don't come cheap."

"I was afraid you'd say that."

"My father has a big floor safe in his office. I've never looked inside it, but I think Desiree knows the combination."

"What makes you think so?"

"She knows everything," Randy said. "After Lupe left, she just moved in and took over."

"It's not hard to see why," Longarm said, remembering that body.

"Desiree is a witch," Randy said. "She is poison."

"Yeah," Longarm agreed with a wink, "but we all have to die sometime."

"She even tried to pull me into her web," Randy confessed, missing Longarm's poor attempt at humor. "Can you believe that? She tried to get me to hump her one day out in the hills."

"Why?"

"It wasn't because of my irresistible good looks and philosophical bent of mind," Randy said. "She's screwing Clyde too. I think she's doing it to use one of us against the other. That's all that I can figure."

"She does sound evil."

170

"You don't know the half of it," Randy said, lapsing into his own deep thoughts. Longarm guessed that the kid had a lot on his mind. Like the killing or arrest of his accursed father and brother and the suffering that they'd inflicted on Lupe Sanchez, Arturo, and his wonderful little family.

"You're in all the way with me, aren't you, Randy?"

"I'm in," he vowed. "I'm in until we either get them or they get us."

"Good," Longarm said as he drummed his heels against the ugly black's ribs and sent it galloping toward Reno with Randy's buckskin matching him stride for stride.

Chapter 17

Marshal Gus Bell hadn't said a word since Longarm and the kid from Helldorado had started to tell their story. But now, with the story finished, he leaned back in his office chair and said, "Friday morning, the Bank of Reno, huh?"

"That's the plan," Longarm said. "It might change, but that's how it stood when we left early yesterday morning."

Bell nodded, and then his gaze settled on Randy. "No double crosses?"

"No," Randy vowed. "But Custis has promised me that there will be no slaughter. He said that my father, brother, and the gang will be given every opportunity to surrender."

"You said that?" the marshal of Reno asked, head swiveling to regard Longarm.

"I did and meant it," Longarm said. "My view is that we let them get into the bank and then we slam the door on them."

"Why wait?" Bell demanded. "If we do that, innocent

bank personnel could get hurt."

"Replace them with local and federal lawmen," Longarm suggested. "We need to actually catch the gang in the act of committing the robbery."

"Why?" Gus asked. "You just said that Randy is willing to testify that the Killion gang was responsible for that train robbery on Donner Pass."

"And what if Randy were to be eliminated?" Longarm asked. "If that happened, our star witness and probably our prosecution's case would vanish like smoke in the wind. We can't win on the basis of one witness anyway. They'll produce other witnesses to say that Matthew Killion and his bunch were seen somewhere else on the day of that train robbery."

"I guess you're right," Bell admitted. "But I sure don't like the idea of using our bank as a shooting gallery."

"We'll do everything possible to avoid that," Longarm said with more assurance than he really felt.

"Okay," Bell said, "I'll start getting help right away and I'll put them in the bank, replacing the regular people."

"Good," Longarm said. "Killion will probably keep a few men outside to watch for trouble and to hold the horses. We need to take care of them and make sure that there is no escape."

"Any ideas?"

"A few," Longarm said. "I'll try and be one of the gang's inside men, and Randy, maybe you can persuade your father to let you stay outside and help hold the horses. As soon as it begins to happen, you can get the drop on the others outside and we can rush them off the street without a shot being fired."

"You make it sound very easy," Randy said.

"It won't be. Whatever can go wrong almost certainly will go wrong. But if we eliminate their means of escape, I'm hoping that they'll just surrender."

"I think you're being wildly optimistic," Gus Bell said. "But I'm going to play it according to your rules. After all, you're the one who's bringing them in to us on a platter."

"Well," Longarm said, extending a hand to Gus, "we'll see you tomorrow morning. Right now, though, we'd better make tracks for Helldorado."

"It's a pretty long ride," Bell said. "You'll almost have to change horses and turn around to be back here by tomorrow morning when the Bank of Reno opens."

"I know that."

Bell frowned. "And it's easy to see that your side wound is paining you, Custis."

"It'll hold up," Longarm said, heading for the door.

He was stopped by Bell's voice. "Oh, by the way, I thought you'd like to know that your Wyoming girl got herself married."

Longarm turned, and a smile touched the corners of his mouth. "Irma got married already?"

"That's right. She's got a husband along with Sam Allen's money and respectability."

"Just keep an eye out in case Irma's past comes riding in to cause her grief," Longarm asked.

"I'll do that," Bell promised. "And about our beautiful Lady Caroline?"

"What about her?"

Gus winked. "I'm taking her out in a surrey to watch the mustangs next week and maybe have a little picnic and whatever else she might want to enjoy."

"Dammit, Gus, I was supposed to do that!"

"Sorry, but Caroline got tired of waiting. We've been out to dinner twice now and she trusts me."

"You sly sonofabitch," Longarm said with annoyance. "You've moved in on my territory."

"You're right," Gus admitted, looking delighted with himself. "Lady Caroline is a remarkable woman, and she is very attracted to a man who carries a badge. We're just getting along swimmingly."

Longarm swore under his breath as he tromped out the door. After they climbed into their saddles, Randy asked, "What was that all about?"

"Lady Caroline."

"What is she, royalty of some kind?"

"That's right," Longarm said, angrily reining his horse into the street. "And if we live through tomorrow, I'll tell you all about her."

Randy looked confused, but Longarm was too pissed off at Marshal Gus Bell to care.

"You sonofabitch!" Killion swore, his fist driving up to connect against the side of Longarm's jaw and send him crashing to the floor.

Stunned, Longarm almost went for his six-gun, but Randy jumped in before his father could kick Longarm in his wounded side. "It was my fault, dammit! I told you that! I'm the one who wanted to go to Virginia City! Not Custis. He just went along for the ride."

"You *knew* we'd planned to rob a bank in Reno tomorrow, didn't you!"

"Yes, Gil told me, but—"

The flat of Matthew Killion's hand smashed into Randy's face. The kid staggered, and Clyde caught

175

and shoved him back at their father. "Kick his uppity educated ass!"

"Shut up!" Killion hissed, turning his rage on his eldest. "Clyde, you're too gawddamn dumb and mean to even be tolerated!"

Clyde, one moment grinning like a fool at the expense of his kid brother, now shrank back, eyes bright and filled with pent-up hatred. "You don't be talking to me like that, Pa! Not in front of everybody!"

Matthew Killion took a menacing step toward his brutish son. "You imbecile! You worthless, bloody . . ."

The words died in his throat as Clyde drew his gun and grinned wolfishly. "You ain't gonna say those things no more about me, Pa! I swear you'll take 'em back right now or I'll send you straight to hell!"

Killion froze. "Put the gun away," he ordered, eyes darting to the other men to see if they would help. But no one moved.

"Apologize, *Mister* Killion," Clyde yelled in a menacing voice, "or I'll drill a hole in you!"

Longarm met Randy's eyes, and they were scared. "Easy," he whispered.

"Apologize, you miserable, weak old sonofabitch!" Clyde screamed at his father.

Killion snapped, "In hell I will!"

Clyde's gun bucked in his fist twice, and Matthew Killion began to stumble back until he crashed over a table.

"Pa!" Randy cried, rushing over to his father.

"He'd lived too long anyway," Clyde said, coming up swiftly behind Randy and pistol-whipping him across the back of the head. Randy grunted and collapsed across his father's body.

Longarm started to go for his six-gun, but he changed his mind as Clyde spun on him and said, "You with us, or against us?"

"With you," Longarm said, knowing he was a hairsbreadth from dying.

Clyde quivered with excitement, and then he looked around at the other outlaws, who were frozen in shock. "The Reno bank job is still on for tomorrow morning," Clyde told them, taking command. "It's all been planned and it's going to happen, only I'm going to give you all bigger shares than my pa would have. Are you boys riding for Clyde Killion now?"

One man finally dipped his chin in assent, then another and another, until they were all nodding.

"Good," Clyde said with satisfaction. "Then we leave Helldorado and ride out at midnight."

Desiree had been watching. Satisfied that a new master had taken control, she sidled over to Clyde, slipped her arm around his thick waist, and pressed her hip against his. "What do you want *me* to do?" she purred.

Clyde practically drooled on her. "You'll pleasure me until midnight, what else?"

She smiled and looked down at the unconscious Randy. "And what about the kid?"

Clyde holstered his gun. "He's gonna *earn* his share this time. He's gonna ride up in the front with the grown men."

"But he's out cold," she said with what she probably thought was a sympathetic tone of voice.

"He'll ride with us at midnight," Clyde vowed. "Either sitting in his saddle or lashed across it. Either way, the fair-haired boy is going to finally get his little hands dirty."

Desiree smiled seductively. Her hand brushed across Clyde's crotch. "Aren't you all done talking yet?" she breathed.

"Yeah," he said, propelling her toward the stairs and his father's office, "we ain't going to talk anymore unless it's you beggin' me for more of my meat."

Desiree laughed shrilly, and Longarm hurried to Randy's side with gunsmoke and death hanging in the air all around them.

Matthew Killion was dead, but what had taken his place was even more evil.

The next morning, the Killion gang drifted into Reno in small groups, no more than three together, and they tied their horses up around the Bank of Reno. Just before entering the town, Longarm had learned that he was to help hold the horses, while Randy was going inside the bank along with Clyde and four others. The remainder of the gang were to just hang around and be ready in case there was any trouble.

"Good luck," Longarm said in a soft voice as Randy headed into the bank.

Randy glanced back at Longarm, and he was obviously scared and unwell. He'd taken a vicious pistol-whipping, and it was a wonder that he was even able to stand up and walk this morning, much less to have endured the long night ride over from Helldorado.

As soon as the door closed behind Randy and the other outlaws, Longarm turned on the other three men holding horses and drew his six-gun.

"Put your hands up and grab saddlehorns," he ordered. "Don't say a word and you might even live to stand trial."

The three outlaws twitched, but when Longarm cocked back the hammer of his Colt, they were quick to follow his orders. At the same time, Gus Bell and his deputies were catching the other outside members of the Killion gang by complete surprise and without a shot being fired.

"Got 'em all!" Bell called out in a low but jubilant voice to Longarm. "Now get 'em off the street and get ready for the ones inside!"

Longarm quickly disarmed his three captives and handed them over to Bell's deputies. He turned to look at the bank door and made his decision. "I'm going in there."

"Are you crazy?"

"They won't realize there's a problem out here," Longarm explained, holstering his gun, "and I want to be close to that kid if lead starts flying."

Bell didn't like it, but he understood. "Just don't be slow to duck."

Longarm went through the bank door. Clyde had his gun trained on the supposed bank personnel, while Randy and the others were stuffing cash into money sacks.

When Randy saw Longarm out of the corner of his eye, he seemed to reach his own decision. He dropped the sack he had been stuffing with greenbacks and went for his six-gun.

"Everyone freeze and nobody gets hurt!" he cried.

Clyde had already caught Randy's sudden movement out of the corner of his eye and was going for his gun. Longarm made a desperate stab for his own weapon.

Randy's Colt bucked first, but Longarm's six-gun barked only a fraction of a second later. The two shots were so tightly spaced that they blended into one. Clyde's shirtfront blossomed crimson. He lifted on his toes and tried to level his gun. Longarm shot the big bastard cleanly between the eyes while the other outlaws clawed for their guns.

During the next few heartbeats, four more members of the Killion gang died, the victims of a fusillade of gunfire from many directions. The wonder, Longarm later was to realize, was that a lot of innocent men were not killed in the heavy crossfire.

"Hold your fire!" Longarm bellowed. "Everyone hold their fire!"

The interior of the Bank of Reno was riddled and choking with acrid gunsmoke. Longarm holstered his gun and rushed over to the kid from Helldorado. "Are you all right?"

"I killed my own brother," Randy whispered.

"You actually missed him," Longarm said. "My bullets brought him down. I put the one between Clyde's eyes."

"You did?"

"Damn right," Longarm said, knowing that he was telling a half truth. Randy's bullet had actually scored first, and would soon have proved fatal if Longarm hadn't drilled Clyde two more times, once through the lung and finally through the brain.

"I'm leaving," Randy said, looking badly shaken. "I'm getting the hell out of this town."

"Where are you going to?"

"To Mormon Station, then Sonora." Randy took a deep breath and fingered his violated scalp. "What about you, Custis?"

"I'm going to Denver. Marshal Bell can arrest Desiree and get her to open your father's safe. I'm finished with

Helldorado. I don't ever want to see the damned place again."

"Me neither," Randy said as they stepped outside to drink in the cool, clean air and leave the killing far behind.

Watch for

**LONGARM AND THE
SILVER MINE MARAUDERS**

197th novel in the bold LONGARM series
from Jove

Coming in May!

A special offer for people who enjoy reading the best Westerns published today.

WESTERNS!

NO OBLIGATION

Mail the coupon below

To start your subscription and receive 2 FREE WESTERNS, fill out the coupon below and mail it today. We'll send your first shipment which includes 2 FREE BOOKS as soon as we receive it.